FIT TO KILL

Tony Duchenne saves the life of Ambrose Halder, the exiled ruler of Sansovino, a small Caribbean island now controlled by Aloysius Morane. Halder wants to square his account with Morane, whatever the cost, and eventually Tony agrees to go to Sansovino to gather information, but soon the action shifts to the tranquil Berkshire countryside. A professional assassin – Bennie Lucas – is called in to take care of Morane. At the last moment Tony has a change of heart and wants to stop the killing, but he is too late – Bennie knows how these matters should be done and Tony Duchenne is merely a spectator.

FIT TO KILL

FIT TO KILL

by

Michael Cronin

Dales Large Print Books
Long Preston, North Yorkshire,
BD23 4ND, England.

British Library Cataloguing in Publication Data.

Cronin, Michael
    Fit to kill.

    A catalogue record of this book is
    available from the British Library

    ISBN   978-1-84262-577-4 pbk

First published in Great Britain in 1976
by Robert Hale & Company

Dales Large Print is an imprint of Library Magna Books Ltd.

Printed and bound in Great Britain by
T.J. (International) Ltd., Cornwall, PL28 8RW

1

Tony Duchenne came from one of the most respected families in Quebec. His father was a partner in a firm of lawyers of high repute and long-standing, and his mother was known for her devotion to the Church and her support of charitable causes; she had a brother who was a bishop, and it was her dearest wish to see her Tony one day following his uncle into the Church.

At school Tony was a good student, quick and intelligent and never in any kind of trouble, and outwardly as pious as his devout parents expected. A son to be proud of.

Without making any parade of being athletic, he was an excellent swimmer and captain of the school tennis team: he preferred singles to doubles, and showed little interest in team games. He was not a mixer, and the normal social activities of the youngsters of his own age and income-group appeared to have no attraction for him. He had no regular girl friends, although he was

7

growing into quite an attractive young man with a thoughtful, sensitive face and curly black hair, and nice manners when he was with a girl even if she didn't matter much.

His father made him a liberal allowance, and he had the frequent use of the family's second car with no questions asked, which was far from being the case with most of his class-mates. Thus he had all the ingredients for a full social life, with the backing of an assured position in local society.

He made little use of his advantages, which made him something of an oddity with his fellows, but then it was pretty widely assumed that he was going into the Church in due course, although nobody ever actually asked him. Not even his mother, she just went on praying that it would happen.

One or two more adventurous girls tried to take him on, but none of them got any-where. He would never be worked into a situation where he would have to do some-thing active, like making a pass at what was on offer. He was polite. Too damn polite. As though what a girl had was something sort of on a pedestal, for God's sake. A girl had to make all the running, and in the end she finished up with a big nothing and thank you for a pleasant evening.

He wasn't a fairy either, that had been well established in the showers at the school gym when he had knocked a hairy senior flat on his butt for making a suggestion.

He had to be ecclesiastical material, sure enough. Otherwise he was quite a nice sort of guy. He was usually top of the class and didn't make any business of it.

As he grew older he never got involved in any drunken escapades, or in any disreputable parties with the kind of girl no decent young man would ever bring home to meet his mother. Sex was something that was never discussed in the Duchenne household, because sex meant marriage, and Tony's parents were of the settled opinion that marriage would not be for him. He was coming up to eighteen, and he was still a virgin. And apparently content to be so.

Then his father's younger sister arrived for an extended visit, and Tony began to grow up in earnest.

Aunt Clothilde was a widow, and a much-travelled lady. She had an elegance and a sophistication that soon fascinated her nephew, because it was his first experience of a world outside the fairly rigid conventions of upper middle class life in Quebec.

9

She had lived in Paris and Rome and London. She had met interesting people, people of importance and culture, and her conversation was sprinkled with famous names and risqué anecdotes if you were quick enough to pick up the clues. It was all done with great charm and verve.

Tony knew that his mother did not approve of Aunt Clothilde, that she considered her too worldly and shallow – a rich woman who had travelled the world amusing herself, probably having *affaires* as well. She had that kind of figure, and the clothes to have men wondering about her, and not wondering in a nice way either. Madame Duchenne would never think of showing herself off the shameful way Clothilde did, all legs and bust, and that talk – as though the world was nothing but a playground for women like her with nothing to do but spend their money on themselves. And make fools of men. Even good decent men wouldn't be safe from her.

After the visit had lasted some weeks and their guest showed no signs of moving on, Madame Duchenne had a few words with her husband. Clothilde was obviously having a bad effect on Tony. He was too taken up with her, and it just wasn't right or healthy for a young man at such an impressionable stage in his life to be spending so much time with a woman like Clothilde, even if she was his aunt. Something would have to be done. She was a bad influence, she was giving him the wrong ideas, and she didn't go to church.

Her husband did not share her alarm. There was no harm in Clothilde, and he thought it quite natural for Tony to be interested in her. She was a good sport, she was full of life and bright ideas and easy to be with, and he certainly was not prepared to tell his only sister that she had outstayed her welcome.

Madame Duchenne took her husband's refusal to do his duty as some kind of a reflection on herself, and there followed one of their infrequent marital wrangles. Clothilde was aware of the discord and secretly found it amusing: it was such a stuffy household, and poor young Tony wasn't being given much of a chance to find out about himself and the kind of man he was likely to be.

Listening to him and watching him, she had come to the conclusion that everybody was wrong in what they expected from him, especially that holy mother of his. Perhaps he didn't even know himself. So maybe he didn't go out with girls and dutifully accompanied his parents to church on Sundays, and he didn't appear to have acquired any bad habits. But Clothilde decided that it would be a great mistake if he went into the Church.

He was no natural celibate. One day he would break out, Clothilde had no doubt about that – he was becoming more and more aware of her as a woman, and when she slipped into the front seat of the car beside him they both knew he was conscious of her nice legs – and they really were still nice legs, well worth looking at.

She knew how to tease him and make him laugh, as though they were both of the same age. He had been brought up to think of sex as something sacred perhaps, or just dirty if it was outside the bonds of matrimony. He knew nothing of women. But his interest was growing.

Clothilde thought of moving out before anything might happen that she might regret. That would be the sensible thing to do. But then she thought how awful it would be if he found out too late that women mattered in his life and he had to become one of those priests who broke their vows and went off with a woman. It might ruin Tony's life if that happened to him.

He must have heard reams of sermons about chastity and purity and so on; it would have been drummed into him from the beginning. And that Canon Rearden from the parish church was in the habit of dropping into the house, and it was Tony he was after. And Tony couldn't possibly know the importance of deciding to live his life apart from all that a woman can bring to a normal healthy man.

He needed guidance, and not the kind of advice he might get from any middle-aged cleric. At least he ought to be given the chance of knowing what he was renouncing.

Clothilde was thirty-eight years old and she had been a widow now for some six years. Her sex life with her husband had been particularly satisfactory, although they had had no children. And since she had become a widow with enough money to go where she pleased, Clothilde had seen no reason to spend every night alone in her bed mourning the dear departed.

There had been just a few discreet liaisons, only one of which had lasted any real length of time; she might even have married the man except that it eventually came to her notice that he had left a wife and two children back in Durban. She had never been promiscuous, and taking another woman's husband had never seemed the right thing to do. She had her private standards, and a man had to be something special before he began to register with her.

Sex was lovely and beautiful. It was the whole point of being alive.

She knew she was not strictly beautiful, but she had the money and the leisure to look after herself, and she could make a striking figure in any assembly.

Her eyes were clear and blue, and there were no tell-tale wrinkles yet; her hair was genuinely blonde, and needed little help to keep its bright sheen; she had quite magnificent legs, and knew how to use them to the best effect.

So it was no wonder that Tony Duchenne was finding her more interesting than any aunt ought to be, and thirty-eight was a good age for a woman to be because it meant she was about at her best, and she would know enough to keep everything under control, most of all when the object of her attentions was twenty years younger.

They had drifted into a delicate situation,

and Clothilde would have been very indignant if anybody had suggested that she had deliberately set out to corrupt and seduce her nephew. He was charming and talented, and she felt it would be such a pity if he docilely settled for the kind of life his family seemed to expect for him.

On the other hand, if he really did have a vocation for the Church, she knew there was nothing she could say or do that would make any difference. She was a casual agnostic herself, but she told herself more than once that she would never do anything to hurt Tony. That would be unpardonable.

There came a week-end when Tony's parents had to be away on a visit to old friends in the country. It was a long-standing invitation, Clothilde didn't know the people and declined to add herself to the party. Tony had a tennis match which he couldn't get out of since it was the important one of the summer and he was the team captain.

The Duchenne domestic staff consisted of a cook and a house-maid, and in the proposed absence of the master and mistress they had been promised extra time off for the week-end, which meant that Tony and Aunt Clothilde would be alone in the house most of the time. Privately Madame Duc-henne thought the arrangement quite im-proper, but she said nothing about it since she knew it would be taken as something of an insult to Clothilde to suggest she couldn't be left alone with her nephew.

That first night they went upstairs together, and, as was her custom, Clothilde gave Tony the kind of quick kiss any respectable lady might give her nephew. She was reading in bed when there was a tap on the door, and Tony came in; he was wearing pyjamas and a dressing-gown.

'May I come in and talk to you for a while?' he said. 'Do you mind?'

She closed her book and patted the side of her bed. 'Is it important, Tony?' she said. 'We've spent a lot of time this evening just talking.'

'I need your advice,' he said, settling himself on the bed. 'I'm in a muddle.'

'You're not going to be a priest,' she said, 'isn't that it?'

He nodded, his face was very serious and unhappy. He wasn't looking at her. 'I don't think I'm worthy, I'd make a mess of it; I've had doubts in my mind for a long time now – do you think I'm being stupid?'

'No,' she said, 'just sensible; it's a big decision, Tony, and I don't think you ought to let anybody else make it for you. You've talked to Canon Rearden about it?'

'Many times,' he said. 'You don't like him very much, do you?'

Clothilde smiled and patted his hand. 'He's a good man, but he doesn't approve of me, I'm afraid.'

'He thinks I'll get over my doubts once I'm at the theological college; he says it's quite normal and nothing to be ashamed of at my age.'

'And that doesn't satisfy you?' she said.

'Not really.' He paused, then looked at her and said, 'I can't stop thinking about women–'

'That isn't so dreadful,' she said.

'It is for a prospective Church student who'll have to live his life with nothing to do with a woman. I'm no saint, and I don't know that I'd ever make a good priest, not like the Canon–'

'Or your uncle the Bishop,' she said, and she smiled. 'You ought to get away from here for a while, right away; give yourself a chance to get things into the right perspective. If you stay here you're going to be swamped.'

'The Canon has suggested a Retreat in a

monastery,' said Tony.

Clothilde laughed. 'That wasn't quite what I had in mind. Quebec isn't the whole world, Tony, and the Canon may not have all the right answers for you. You could take a university course somewhere abroad, you ought to meet other young people with different ideas and ambitions, that would be a real test of whether you have a vocation for the Church or not.'

'I'd like that,' he said slowly. 'But my father would never allow it. I've been reading a lot about the School of Economics in London; I'd like to go there.'

'Well, that's certainly no monastery from all I hear,' said Clothilde cheerfully, 'but I'm sure it would be good for you, broaden your horizon and so on – if you came out of there with a good degree and you still wanted to be a priest you would be all the better for it, better equipped to deal with unbelievers, like me.'

She smiled and took his hand in hers. 'Would you like me to talk to your father about it?'

'Even if he agreed,' said Tony, 'the others would get at him and stop me from going: mother and the Canon–'

'Not forgetting the bishop,' said Clothilde.

'We have some heavy opposition, but let me have a go at your father, he generally listens to me.'

'You're a pretty marvellous person,' said Tony. 'I never thought a woman could be so understanding.'

'Approximately half the population of the world is female,' said Clothilde. 'We can't all be morons, we do have a clue here and there, my dear Tony: male and female, He created them, and I think it's a pretty good arrangement.'

'I've never really seen a woman,' he said. 'Except statues.'

'You know the essentials,' she said. 'Now, it's getting late and I think you ought to be off to your own bed. I may be an evil woman, but the sexual education of my nephew does not fit in with my personal scheme of things.'

He lifted her hand and kissed it. 'I think of you an awful lot,' he said.

'I should hope so indeed,' she said. 'No woman likes to be ignored.'

'You're beautiful! When you're in the room I can't see anybody else.'

Clothilde sat up straight in bed; her night-dress was transparent and low cut. 'Look at me, Tony,' she said softly. 'You are making me ashamed of myself.'

He reached out and began to stroke her shoulder very gently.

'I have never seen anything so lovely,' he said in a small dreamy voice.

'You want to make love to me,' she said harshly. 'You think that's what I'm waiting for? Tony, Tony, just think a minute – this is all wrong for both of us, you are making me feel like a whore … look–'

She slipped out on the other side of the bed, whipped her nightdress over her head and tossed it away. With her hands at her sides she stood there.

'That's what a woman looks like,' she said. 'Now leave me and go to bed, Tony, before you shame the pair of us.'

'Now I know how beautiful you are,' he said thoughtfully, 'I will never be able to forget it.'

'This is no lifeless statue,' she said. 'If it is wicked to show myself, then I am wicked.'

'Please stay there,' he whispered. 'I don't want to touch you, I only want to look at you.' He hadn't moved from the bed.

She raised both hands, palms uppermost, as though making an offering. She thought of cupping her breasts. But that would be too crude. There was a rapt smile on his face.

'Enough,' she said. She turned and walked into the connecting bathroom and closed the door. And she knew that if he had come across to her and taken her in his arms it would have happened – and with her own nephew!

He sat on the edge of the crumpled bed, with the sheets still perfumed from her body, and he took his head at the wonder of it all, her jutting breasts that seemed to have a life of their own, and the grace of her moving hips and legs as she walked out of his sight. This was what the poets wrote about – and the moral theologians condemned down the ages … the sins of the flesh.

He went back to his own room, like a man in a dream. It was too disturbing for sleep, or prayers that night. It was delicious torment that was going to give him no peace. Canon Rearden would have apoplexy – and if his mother ever knew…

And for Clothilde also it was a restless night. She was not proud of what had happened. She had acted on impulse, and she knew it was time for her to move before any real damage was done.

In the middle of the following afternoon there was a phone call that solved their problems in the most definitive and tragic

21

manner. A burst tyre at high speed had sent the Duchenne car over the edge of the road and down into a steep ravine, the car had caught fire and both bodies had been burnt beyond recognition.

Clothilde delayed her departure, naturally. There was so much to be done, and Tony needed her now more than ever. During the night after they had buried his parents and all the mourning party, including the Bishop, had departed, Tony came to her room, and this time she did not turn him away. She would never be ashamed of that night. It was never repeated.

Two months later, when Tony travelled to London to begin the autumn term at the School of Economics, Clothilde accompanied him and helped him to find a flat. They settled on a flat in a mews near Hyde Park; it had room enough for two, but there was never any suggestion on either side that she should move in with him and pretend to be his housekeeper. Clothilde prudently stayed in a hotel in Knightsbridge.

Financially Tony was in an enviable position; while his father's estate was being wound up he had more than enough money available for his needs; he could live where

and how he chose; he would be no impover-
ished student struggling along from term to
term on a grant.

London was full of possibilities for a young
man with a pleasant appearance and ample
money in his pocket, and it was soon clear
to Aunt Clothilde that Tony wasn't going to
need her guiding hand much longer. He had
slipped into his new mode of life without
any fuss, and if he continued to go to church
he kept it pretty much of a secret.

He was working hard and was soon
actively involved in student societies, and
his flat became a popular gathering place in
the evenings and at week-ends; he was a
good host, one of the very few younger men
with the right sort of pad and plenty of
coffee and drinks and no nonsense about
bringing your own bottle. He was a persuasive talker and liked being surrounded
by a noisy audience of his own kind – the
bright young people who knew they had the
solutions to the world's problems.

Clothilde still visited him periodically, and
she was interested to notice that not all of his
friends were male. To her most of the girls
seemed incredibly self-assured and clever,
and she wondered if Tony had done any

experimenting privately with any of them. He didn't confide in her any longer, although he was still charmingly polite when she appeared. He was changing very rapidly, and Quebec was a long way behind him now.

Tony had been launched, and he seemed very happy with the course he had taken, so Clothilde set out on her travels once more, and she had to admit that she was not altogether easy in her mind about the way things might go with Tony.

There was a basic flaw in his character, she concluded. Perhaps it was that he had always been too docile, too superficial, without a mind of his own. Well, all that was certainly changing now.

She spent the winter with some friends near San Remo. At first she heard from Tony fairly regularly, chatty little letters, amusing, and really telling her not much about himself. They read like the letters of a playboy. Lots of fun and crazy parties. London was a great place, and he was evidently enjoying it.

During the Easter vacation he flew to Quebec and visited his parents' graves, then he had some lengthy sessions with his father's executors. There was not going to be as much money as most people had expected from the estate: the Duchennes had been living up to the limit of their income, and it appeared that Tony's father had uncharacteristically made some unwise investments in recent years.

However, Tony would have enough left to assure him of a reasonable private income, but against the advice of his father's former partners he had some of the investments converted into cash and transferred to a London bank where he could get at it. About his plans for the future he was vague and uncommunicative. He might go into public service, politics, something like that, after he had taken his degree. But first of all he intended to travel and see more of the world.

He visited few of his old friends, and none of the clergy who were still ready to call him back to the fold, especially Canon Rearden, who made several attempts to talk to him about his future and his spiritual welfare, in vain. This was a very different Tony Duchenne from the earnest youth who had listened so obediently in the past and from whom such excellent things were expected. It made the Canon very sad to think of what a loss the Church had sustained when this promising young disciple had turned his back on all he once held so dear.

Tony returned to London and that was the

last Quebec saw of him. London was his chosen scene and there was so much he intended to do. During that summer Clothilde went on a leisurely tour of Austria and Italy with her San Remo friends. In Florence she met Henry Furnivall. He was in the middle fifties, a widower, and of independent means. A handsome man, cultured and with a delightful sense of humour.

He found Clothilde entrancing. He didn't want to live with her, which she was quite ready to do. He wanted to marry her.

Clothilde gave it serious thought, and decided it would be a pleasant change to be made into an honest woman once more. Henry adored her and knew how to keep her happy. He had been a widower for many years, so there would be no shadow of another woman to come between them.

He had a villa at Capri, and extensive farming interests dotted about here and there, including some profitable vineyards near Cape Town.

They were married in Rome. She sent Tony an invitation to the wedding, but the date clashed with some important examinations he had to take. He had a silver tea service air-freighted as a present, with his best wishes.

After that Clothilde heard very little from Tony, which was rather what she expected, and wanted.

They met only once more after that, over a year later when Henry had to visit London on business. The three of them dined together, but the evening was not a huge success. To Tony the man Clothilde had married was just another rich farmer, and Henry found Tony brash and opinionated. And Clothilde was relieved when the evening was over, and nobody made any attempt to follow it up, although Clothilde and her husband were staying in London for a full week.

When she thought about it, and she did think about it from time to time, Clothilde found it hard to believe that she had once shown herself naked to Tony. What a bizarre episode that had been. And no credit to her.

She didn't think he would content himself now with just looking. Did he even remember what she had looked like?

It was as well that she had made her home in South Africa with her Henry, because that young man could be dangerous still if she was silly enough to see much of him. Nephew or no nephew.

2

Tony graduated with first-class honours, and acquired some academic awards as well, so that he was admitted to be one of the outstanding graduates of his year. Although he was not exactly in the market for a job, the personnel director of at least one international concern invited him for an interview.

Tony presented himself, listened attentively to the glittering career that might lie ahead of him if he made the grade, and then shattered the interviewer by giving him a crisp and highly intelligent criticism of his firm's recent policy in its overseas operations, ending with some succinct suggestions that indicted how little he thought of the various members of the board.

It was breath-taking in its impertinence, and disconcerting in its accuracy. While the personnel expert was still collecting himself, Tony politely took his leave. It had been an interesting experience.

He got himself involved in the fringes of the television world, and did some research on a free-lance basis for one of the independent companies; current affairs programmes and documentaries. He enjoyed it for a while, working under pressure and mixing with the professionals in a production team. But he was never really willing to submit himself to the disciplines that would make for success in such a competitive field. He had that comforting cushion of private means to fall back on, so it made little difference to him if a project fell down and there was no work and no money coming in.

He was living in a style that suited him, and his social life was active and very satis-factory. There was no one special girl friend, and he was always careful not to let any girl imagine she had any particular claim on him. He enjoyed their company, but if any girl showed signs of going broody on him, and some of them did because he was defin-itely a good catch, he would contrive not to be alone when she called – or just on the way out when she rang. There is nothing so elusive as a young man who does not intend to be hooked.

If any of his assorted group of females ever

spent a night at his flat, nobody ever seemed to know about it, although there was naturally some speculation, both male and female.

Tony was fun all right, but there was something about him that puzzled most of his friends. You could never really feel that you had got through to him. Even after a few drinks, when inhibitions should have been loosened, Tony retained a reserve that gave away nothing about his real self.

He would disappear for weeks on end without warning, travelling on his own and without any set plan, just idling his time as though waiting for something to happen to his life. Seeing new places and meeting new people.

Just for the hell of it he submitted a series of articles to one of the travel agency periodicals. They had a flavour all of their own, and he had done them largely for his own amusement. They were well received and he was invited to supply more in the same vein.

As a result he met Angus Menzies, who was already in the travel business as a junior executive and knew all the business end of it. He had been some three years ahead of Tony at the L.S.E., and he had ideas about starting a small agency to offer a specialised service – travel off the beaten track for discerning travellers; every detail to be thoroughly researched in person by one of the principals; no cut-rate package deals; individual attention – exclusive and expensive, only for people with some notion of culture, and an intelligent appreciation of what faraway places might have to offer.

With the right publicity it might catch on, and at least one of the bosses would have to be on the move, doing the field work.

It was a gamble, but Tony was interested. Angus Menzies had no capital. Tony supplied enough to keep them afloat for a year, and they were in business. They rented a small office in Victoria, and spent rather more than they could afford on a publicity campaign. A trickle of clients began to arrive, although not enough to cover their overheads, and there were all the headaches incidental to setting up a new business in the face of stiff competition, and with limited resources.

However, they plugged away, and for the first time in his adult life Tony Duchenne found himself totally involved in something that made serious demands on his energy and initiative. He did all the travelling, and every hotel quoted in their brochures had been vetted and sampled personally by Tony.

It was an expensive way of operating a business, but it was beginning to pay off.

After some prolonged negotiations he had concluded a vary satisfactory arrangement with a beautiful little country establishment just outside San Juan in Puerto Rico. Jorge and Isabella Uragon were the proprietors. Isabella was a handsome woman in the middle thirties, and her husband was some years older. They had no children, and before Tony had been in the hotel long he knew that Isabella was a discontented wife who found life with her husband less than exhilarating. It was potentially a dangerous situation, because Isabella made it embarrassingly clear that she thought Tony attractive, and she was not being too subtle about it.

During Tony's last night with them, Jorge Uragon said he had a long-standing poker session that needed his attention, with some *compadres* in a San Juan club. It would probably last all night, but he would return in time to see Tony off in the morning.

Tony was well asleep that night when he awoke to discover he was not now alone.

Isabella had slipped in beside him, and she was stripped for the serious business so that she appeared all arms and legs and scented breath.

'Make love to me,' she demanded. She was climbing all over him and there was plenty of her and all of it was actively directed at him.

She silenced his faint protests with her avid mouth and her hair was all over his face. 'You make a baby for me,' she said. 'I need a baby...'

It was a difficult invitation to refuse in the circumstances, and Tony tried in vain to think of a way out without offending her. This was women's lib operating with a vengeance, strictly for procreation – Tony Duchenne the almost reluctant stud.

Isabella insisted on a repeat performance because they had a long night in front of them, and she enjoyed showing this shy young man the best ways to please a woman in bed. They would have plenty of time for sleeping afterwards.

Unfortunately the poker session had ended unseasonably early, and Jorge Uragon had burst in on them. He was fairly drunk and very angry and he had a revolver with which he intended to revenge his honour.

Isabella deftly slid out of the line of fire, but Tony was too slow and drowsy. Jorge fired two shots, the first hit the ceiling, but the second got Tony's leg instead of the intimate parts, and he rolled off the bed in a fainting condition, certain that his end had come, and terrified beyond measure.

There was shouting, and another shot so near that he felt the bed jump under the impact and his mouth was full of bile. This was death.

Isabella got to her feet. Naked and unashamed, she went for her husband, wrenched the gun out of his fist, and slapped his face. And Tony floated off into unconsciousness.

He spent three expensive months in hospital, and he very nearly lost a leg. He would limp for the rest of his life, and for the rest of his life the sound of a gun going off or a car back-firing was enough to give him the jitters.

It was the traumatic experience of his life, and all because he hadn't had the wit to say no to the lady while there was time. It was to become his recurring nightmare in the months that followed, waking him all sweaty and trembling in his bed. During those weeks in hospital, with the bills mounting at an alarming rate, he had no visit from Isabella, which did not grieve him too much. Her husband's lawyers were sending him intimidating letters concerning the legal redress that Senor Jorge would take in due course.

The Duchenne future looked bleak indeed. Angus Menzies put in a belated appearance when Tony was hopping along on a crutch in the hospital grounds, and he was of little comfort to the invalid.

This distressing affair had done the firm no good. They depended on goodwill, mutual trust and so forth, and some influential hoteliers had already crossed them off their list: how could you deal with a firm one of whose partners might seduce your womenfolk as soon as your back was turned?

According to the version that Jorge Uragon was putting about, Tony Duchenne was a dangerous sex maniac, and no decent woman would be safe in his company.

Tony found this picture of himself amusing, since Isabella had made all the overtures, but Angus was far more concerned about the damage to the public reputation of the firm. It was likely to prove a costly romp in bed by his injudicious partner, and Angus didn't think it was at all amusing to lose money in this sloppy fashion.

Tony was in no mood to take any more criticism. There were some heated exchanges, and when Angus Menzies finally left the island their partnership was as good as over. Tony might get some of his investment back, but when everything had been settled up there might not be much, and the hospital authorities demanded payment before he was released. So he had to draw on his dwindling capital.

He flew to Jamaica and gave himself a long convalescence. To hell with the travel agency business. He soaked up the sun and he swam and his limp improved. And he met Teresa Sylvester.

She was just a year younger than he was, sun-tanned and athletic, with glossy black hair and lambent dark eyes, and a great appetite for living. She was a native islander but with enough blood from her Dutch ancestors to pass for white. She was a graceful mover on the dance floor, a strong swimmer almost good enough to keep pace with Tony … a laughing girl on a sunlit beach, without a care in the world beyond her own fun, straight out of the pages of a travel brochure.

But not quite.

Teresa had been at school in New Orleans when her mother died, and she had been brought up by her father. He had died a year ago, leaving her the sole owner of a small but flourishing hotel on the island. She had also inherited her father's manager, a Howard Foster, and she soon had reason to believe that Foster had his hand in the till; padding the hotel accounts and taking a rake-off from some of their suppliers.

Tony had moved into the hotel, and he knew enough about the business to share Teresa's suspicions about her manager. Howard Foster was smart and voluble, and very ostentatious about the long hours he was putting in on the job to assist the inexperienced daughter of his late boss. He liked to see to each detail himself, and he became uneasy when Teresa started checking on her own account.

There were discrepancies in the bar takings, and some of the catering overheads didn't bear close examination. A long-term fiddle had been in operation. Howard Foster had been milking the business, and he hadn't been too clever about it because the risk had been negligible once the old man was dead.

When Teresa challenged him, he was at first hurt and on his dignity, but when she enlisted Tony's support with the evidence he had collected, Howard Foster was relieved to be permitted to pack his bags and avoid being prosecuted. Which left Teresa without a manager.

Tony stayed on at the hotel. He had nothing else in view just then, and Jamaica is not the worst place to pass a season in. From time to time he gave Teresa the benefit of his advice, and when she got into a tangle over her paperwork he sorted it out for her.

She thought he was rather marvellous, and that limp he would never explain gave him an extra romantic appearance. He was moreover an absolute gentleman, not like most of the crude young men she had been associating with, who were only after one thing. Tony was different. All the staff liked him because he always had such nice manners.

After that near catastrophe with Isabella, Tony had promised himself that he would be extra cautious in future with any woman under the age of eighty or so. And Teresa, delightful though she surely was, would be no exception. He preserved his chastity for two whole months, during which time he had ample evidence that Teresa would not slap his face if he made a serious pass.

He really felt it was time to be moving. They had rooms on the same floor, and when he was helping her with her accounts they were often alone together into the night, and she did not believe in wearing too many clothes late at night. She was disturbing his sleep, and she knew precisely what effect she was having on him.

One beautiful moonlit night there was a beach barbecue, with buckets of drink and guitars and some nude bathing. All very hilarious and uninhibited under the palms, with Teresa and Tony pairing-off as a natural twosome as the night progressed. The atmosphere was made for loving and they found their own private paradise under the moon. Flesh and blood could stand only so much, and everybody else was similarly engaged.

Six weeks later Teresa told him the news. She was pregnant and she wasn't going to get rid of the baby. He behaved like the perfect gentleman she knew he was. Neither of them wanted a church wedding with all the frills, so they were married quietly in the registrar's office and left on a short honeymoon before the happy news got about.

The Duchenne pilgrimage might well have ended here. They appeared to be a well-matched couple, and plenty of young men on the island envied Tony his undeserved good fortune. Teresa was a real smasher, and she had that nice little hotel business to make her even sweeter.

Their honeymoon on a luxury beach a short plane ride from Kingston was a torrid interlude of sun-bathing and love-making, and Teresa lasted the course much better than Tony did. Her talent for sex was remarkable, and she had no silly ideas about not taking the initiative. Morning, noon, and night, Teresa was ready and in the most devastating fashion, frequently with a coarseness and a lack of finesse that Tony found more than he could cope with.

While she blossomed he wilted, and she teased him and accused him of not loving her properly, and he longed to be in a bed on his own and a good night's sleep. She had to

41

be told over and over how adorable and absolutely fascinating she was, and what a magnificent body she had, and how lucky he was to have her all to himself. She would parade around their bedroom, exhibiting herself and admiring herself in the mirrors, and he thought of Aunt Clothilde and her harmless display all those years ago.

There was nothing about a woman that he needed so urgently to look at now, and there was no magic about the reality – no mystery and no shame. Teresa gloried in being female, and he had to worship at her shrine.

The honeymoon ecstasy tapered off a little when they returned to the hotel. They had a business to attend to. Tony had plans to improve their amenities, and used some of his own money to refurnish a few of the rooms. It helped him to feel he had a stake in the place, and he had already taken over the managerial responsibilities.

Then Teresa's pregnancy proved to be a false alarm, and the quarrels began. Tony found her outbursts of petulance about trivialities unreasonable and told her to get a grip on herself. She was a young woman and they could have other children.

She sulked, called him a selfish pig and

other unpleasantnesses, as though he had been guilty of some heinous offences. There were nights when he found himself impotent in bed with her, and she screamed and stormed at him like a savage until he was obliged to remove himself to another room.

She was spending more and more time out of the hotel, back to her old friends, the beach loungers. One night she returned very late and not at all sober, and the hotel was full of guests.

Somebody had told her what had happened with Isabella and Jorge Uragon in Puerto Rico, and she made a noisy scene right there on the main corridor, with interested guests watching and listening at their doors.

He had married her under false pretences, he was nothing but a lecherous bastard and she was sorry she had ever set eyes on him, and much more in the same vein and at the top of her voice.

Tony slapped her against the wall and unwisely tried to exert some of the traditional French-Canadian marital discipline. She kicked him in the privates and tore at his hair, and the watching guests looked on. This was an odd way for the proprietors of a respectable establishment to carry on.

They slept apart that night, as they had been doing for the past few weeks. This was open war. She ought to see a doctor and get herself straightened out. He spent a long time that night just staring out at the hotel garden and wondering how in the world things had gone so sour. She had become a different woman.

The next morning he didn't catch sight of her until later; he was busy in the office when he saw her drive off in the car they shared. He had a rush of work to do, since several guests had decided to leave and their accounts had to be made up; it was a minor exodus, and he didn't have to guess at the reason for it.

Before lunch he had time to reflect on his position, and he could see little future in it. If anybody had been tricked into marriage he thought he had been the one. If she hadn't thought she was pregnant he would never have married her, he was quite sure of that now. Perhaps she had made a genuine mistake, but was there anything left between them worth salvaging? He was not inclined to make the effort, because she had changed so radically.

If he had really loved her it would be different. He sat at the office desk and added up what he reckoned he had spent of his own money on the hotel, and then drew a cheque on the hotel account to cover it. He left her a brief note telling her about the money and wishing her better luck next time. He was removing himself from a situation that he found intolerable.

He packed the bare essentials in a couple of cases. He would be travelling light, and not by any of the normal exits from the island. If Teresa came looking for her absconding husband he was not going to make it easy for her. He cashed the cheque in Kingston and made his way down to the docks.

Before the afternoon was over he had made a satisfactory deal with the skipper of a small coasting vessel trading among the islands. The M.V. *Gabriella* was smelly and slow, with rough accommodation, indifferent food, and a fairly elastic schedule of calls at the smaller islands.

The crew of four, and the skipper, showed little interest in their passenger; he would have his own reasons for travelling the way he did; maybe he was a little crazy, but when they put in anywhere and there were drinks to be bought he didn't mind putting his hand in his pocket; not a bad feller.

Tony let his beard grow, and adapted himself to this new way of living without much trouble; the physical discomfort was a small price to pay for the feeling of liberation he was enjoying, and he was in no hurry to get anywhere special.

The *Gabriella* nosed her leisurely way through the islands in Grand Cayman and Little Cayman. There were some furtive night calls at quiet bays where nobody showed any lights and the visitors came out in motor boats, and the skipper made it clear to Tony that this was private business and he should stay in his bunk and know nothing. Illicit transactions were taking place and they did not concern the passenger.

On the infrequent occasions when harbour officials were about, Tony took good care to remain invisible just in case anybody became inquisitive. He finally parted company with the *Gabriella* at Punta Gorda because that was as far west as she was going, and he had decided that Mexico might be the right place for him temporarily.

He had never done any business there, and it was very unlikely that Teresa would trace him that far, supposing she was looking for him. There would be plenty of tourists, and the expatriates who had good reason for not living in their native lands – the high-powered defaulters who had got away with the loot. He could lose himself there with ease.

Before he left the skipper of the *Gabriella* introduced Tony to a friend of his who ran a slightly better ship, the *Southern Queen*, bound eventually for Veracruz. Tony was taken on and given the status of deck-hand, unpaid, the understanding being that he would jump ship at Veracruz, and his defection would not be reported to the authorities.

For a price, cash down, he was provided with bogus papers in case he ran into any patrol. He was discovering that living on the shady side could have its expensive periods. The *Southern Queen's* skipper was a mercenary character and gave nothing for nothing, but he kept to their bargain and put Tony ashore at Veracruz at the right place not to be noticed by any official.

He took a room at a quiet place well clear of the docks, and the next day he was on the up-country bus, along with a load of sight-seeing passengers, with whom he thought he was merging very nicely.

There was nothing whatever to connect

him with Teresa in Jamaica; not even a happy memory. His plans were vague. He could stop where he liked and as long as he liked. He could be a genuine tourist. There was plenty worth looking at: Chichen Itza, the pyramids at Palenque, and the magnificent ruins that were being excavated by the archaeologists and their teams of holiday students.

It was all being written up and by professional experts, of course, but he just might hit on an angle all of his own. He had done it before, and it might give some kind of purpose to his travels. If he could sell a couple of articles it would help his finances, and money had begun to figure in his calculations.

He caught a bad dose of 'Montezuma's Revenge' after some suspicious fish dish eaten in a wayside café when he had taken a room near Tlaloc, and it left him weak and inclined to do nothing for a while but look after himself. The heat was fierce, and it should be better down by the coast.

3

Travelling by easy stages he reached Acapulco, the fun city by the sea for the very
rich, which did not include Tony Duchenne.
He had a long and tiresome search before
he found a place with a room to suit his
purse, and after a few days he knew this was
not for him. The time had come to sit down
and have a long think about what was to
happen next.

One tranquil evening he was making his
way innocently along a tree-lined avenue in
the suburbs where there were a few other
strollers. He was about to overtake a tall
elderly gentleman on the pavement when he
noticed a car slowing up alongside. He saw
the young man at the rear window of the
car, and very vividly indeed he was aware of
what that man was holding in his hand, and
it was pointing at Tony because Tony was on
the outside of the pavement.

The sight of a gun being pointed in his
direction from just a few yards away filled
Tony with instant terror. He went plunging

to the pavement, and he took the elderly gentleman with him – he had to, because the old man was in the way. Nothing and nobody would have stopped Tony's dive for self-preservation, and there wasn't even time to scream.

The gun chattered viciously, splitting the evening air. Bullets pinged and whipped across the pavement, and Tony cringed, and into his terrified mind there flashed the overwhelming thought that this was a crazy way to die – shot down by somebody he didn't even know.

The shooting stopped as abruptly as it had started. There was shouting, and women screaming, and the sound of a car leaving at high speed. Tony didn't dare lift his head. He was rigid on top of the old man. He had tried to shrink himself so as to diminish the target area, and his eyes were still shut against the onset of sudden death. Underneath him the old man was beginning to stir, and feet were hurrying along the pavement towards them.

It was then that a fit of trembling gripped Tony, beyond his control. Those who had arrived first at the scene of the action had thought both men must be dead, but then they noticed the trembling, and somebody said dead bodies didn't move. So they eased him off the old man whose life he had so gallantly protected, and they sat him up. Tony got his eyes open. He stopped trembling, he was sick instead, which everybody found very understandable.

The elderly gentleman appeared surprisingly agile after his violent contact with the pavement. He got to his feet without assistance. He dusted himself off, and he actually was offering to help Tony to his feet.

'Sir,' he announced, 'you are a brave man. Those bullets were intended for me. But for you I would now be a dead man – Ambrose Halder thanks you for his life.'

He had got Tony up on his feet, and he embraced him, which saved Tony the embarrassment of falling flat on his face because his legs were still not ready to do their job. There were murmurs of approval from the spectators, and with difficulty Tony stopped himself from spewing again, which would have ruined the image of instant heroism that he had acquired.

His vision cleared, there were people to lean against. Nobody minded. He found his voice. 'That was a near thing,' he said, almost quoting Wellington after Waterloo. 'Lucky for us he wasn't much of a shot.'

'It was your intelligent reaction that saved us,' said Ambrose Halder. He held Tony's right hand in both of his. 'Allow me to congratulate you on your presence of mind, my dear sir. I am eternally in your debt.'

Tony Duchenne shrugged, like one who did this kind of thing every other day. Some of the spectators were pointing out the marks where the bullets had scored the paving stones, and they hadn't been all that far from where Tony had flattened himself on top of the old man.

He had acted in simple panic, and he was a hero. He looked at the man whose life he appeared to have saved. Ambrose Halder was tall and well-built, probably nearing sixty years old; he had a smooth coffee-coloured skin and a commanding nose – aristocratic grey hair, and a small grey goatee beard. Clearly a man of consequence, quite apart from being a man some people disliked enough to take shots at in the street.

'Did you know that man in the car?' said Tony. 'The one with the gun?'

'Ah, my dear sir,' said Ambrose Halder, 'that is a very good question – some ruffian no doubt. I was unable to see his face owing to your prompt action, for which I can never thank you enough.'

A police car arrived. There was an elegant young lieutenant and a brace of constables, and they were prepared to push the noisy crowd around with some strong-arm stuff, and then the lieutenant recognised the tall figure of Ambrose Halder, and things became correct.

There were voluble offerings from some of the bystanders, but little agreement about the car the shots had come from, its colour or make or how many men had been in it. And all Tony Duchenne could say was that he thought the car had been an American model, dark blue or black, and quite new. And the man with the gun? Young, he thought, swarthy, with black hair – a description that could fit every other young man in the city.

The lieutenant did not seem unduly worried about the lack of helpful details. He had a whispered consultation with Ambrose Halder, and as a result Tony Duchenne was invited to join them in the police car.

The two constables were left on the pavement, and the lieutenant drove, but not to the police office to make formal statements, as Tony had been expecting. Senor Ambrose Halder clearly rated preferential treatment.

They drove south of the town, and

stopped at a gate below a pink-washed villa on a spur of cliff. The lieutenant parked the car at the gate, and Halder led them up a steep pathway with wide steps between beds of flowers. The villa itself was perched high up on the cliff, remote and isolated, and not all that easy to find; it was not one of the new luxury residences, with their patios and swimming pools and landscaped grounds.

By the time they had finished with the steps Tony Duchenne was out of breath, and his lame leg began to act up. Ambrose Halder looked as though he could go on climbing those steps for ever.

'Do forgive me,' he said. 'I am used to this climb, but I see your leg pains you–'

'It's nothing,' said Tony.

'An old wound, perhaps?' said Halder. 'You have been a military man, Mr Duchenne?'

Tony Duchenne smiled, and the lieutenant gave him a sharp glance, as though storing something up for future reference.

They went inside, into a long cool shaded room, with a red and white checked floor and coloured mats; the furniture was heavy and dark, in the Spanish colonial style; there was an air of austerity about the room, like the visitors' parlour in a well-endowed religious house. Everything was polished, as though rarely used.

Ambrose Halder turned to Tony and said with a graceful gesture, 'My house is your house, Mr Duchenne. What I have is yours. Will you please make yourself comfortable while the lieutenant and I talk a little?'

'Of course.' Tony selected the least straight-backed of the chairs and sat down. There were no flowers in the room, plenty in the beds outside.

Halder and the lieutenant had gone into another room, and Tony could hear the broken murmur of their voices, and later the faint tinkle of a telephone, and he guessed it might be the lieutenant talking to the police office – a case of attempted murder on a public street ought to arouse some official activity, and so far it seemed to be receiving rather off-hand treatment.

And Ambrose Halder himself had taken it all with unusual calmness for a man of his advanced years. Tony lit a cigarette, he could see nothing that looked like an ashtray, so he put the cigarette out, got up and began a leisurely inspection of the room.

The big feature was the wide picture window that gave a panoramic view of the sea. Whoever had built the villa must have chosen that location because of the view, which was quite breath-taking. Or perhaps he had preferred living in an inaccessible place with no near neighbours. A rich eccentric. It must have cost a packet to get lighting and water up there.

The view was attractive enough now, on a placid sunny evening, with a wonderful shading of colours on the sea, and some sailing craft still out there and in no hurry. In bad weather with a high wind it would be frightening.

There was a handsome cabinet with an assortment of drinks, and he was happy to recognise some bottles of 'Johnny Walker'; the establishments he had been patronising recently had some odd notions of what real Scotch should be. In spite of Halder's invitation to treat the house as his own, he decided to wait for the return of his host.

There were a few pictures on the walls, dark oils in heavy gilt frames, all of them of a vaguely religious character, saints whose names he had forgotten, reminding him of his mother's old sitting-room back in Quebec.

He was wondering what the effect would be if he told Halder the truth – that the very sight of a gun pointed at him would fill him always with panic, that it hadn't been an act of heroism that had sent both of them flat on that pavement with the bullets whipping about them.

He was a complete fraud. Could he tell the old boy that the gallant Tony Duchenne was nothing but a jelly when anybody pointed a gun near him? It would be much simpler to let Halder go on believing that he had been saved from sudden death by a courageous stranger.

Ambrose Halder returned.

'Do forgive me,' he said, 'but you know how fussy these young police officers can be when anything out of the ordinary has happened.'

'I would say it was more than that,' said Tony. 'That was attempted murder, surely. Won't I have to make a statement? After all, I was there.'

'Indeed you were, and it was most fortunate for me that you were,' said Halder, smiling. 'Now what will you drink, Mr Duchenne?'

'Scotch, please,' said Tony. 'Won't the police be doing anything? I don't plan to be in Mexico much longer.'

'They will make their routine enquiries,' said Halder. 'Water or soda?'

'A little water, thank you.'

Halder brought the drinks over, whisky for himself as well. 'You are just a visitor here then?' he said. 'By yourself?'

'I'm on my own. A tourist, if you like.'

'It's pleasant to be young and free to go where one chooses,' said Halder. 'One never knows what will come next.'

'There is that about it,' said Tony.

'The spirit of adventure,' said Halder.

'Not too much of that,' said Tony. 'I prefer to travel peacefully.'

'And your next port of call?'

'I haven't decided.'

'I envy you,' said Halder. 'No responsibilities, no ties? At liberty to follow your own fancy?'

'Within sensible limits,' said Tony. 'I am not in the position to throw money about.'

'Quite,' said Halder. He thought for a moment, gazing at the whisky he had yet to drink. 'Mr Duchenne, I have a suggestion: if you are in no great hurry to leave Mexico, I would consider it a privilege if you would be my guest, here, for as long as you cared to stay.'

'Well, I must say that is a very friendly offer.'

'You would be doing me a favour,' said

Halder. 'I have a car which would be at your disposal, I do little driving myself in these days. I walk for exercise, regularly, which is how I happened to be on foot this evening.'

'You'll have to change your habits a little,' said Tony. 'It was you they were shooting at, wasn't it?'

'It was a political matter,' said Halder. 'There was no harm done, thanks to you. So may I offer you the hospitality of my house, Mr Duchenne?'

'You make it difficult for me to refuse,' said Tony.

'You feel I might prove dangerous company?' said Halder, smiling. 'I am not always a target, believe me. I am sixty years old, and I expect to live many more years.'

The prospect of saving on his hotel expenses for a while Tony Duchenne found attractive. Also this courtly old man interested him; not many men of his age could treat an attempt at murder quite so lightheartedly.

'We should become better acquainted,' said Halder. 'I feel I owe it to myself, and I entertain few visitors here of late ... perhaps you would find it dull? You did me a great service, and now here I am presuming even further on your good nature.'

'It's nothing like that,' said Tony.

'Then it is settled,' said Halder briskly. 'You have your luggage at a hotel? If you will let me have the address I will have it collected.'

'I travel light,' said Tony.

'The only way when one is young,' said Halder. 'As one gets older life becomes more cluttered.'

'I just have one case,' said Tony, 'I've been travelling by bus, and they don't welcome trunks and so forth. I think I'd better collect the case myself, it isn't packed – I wasn't expecting to move quite so quickly.'

'As you wish,' said Halder. 'You might have difficulty in finding this place again, so I will have one of my men drive you.'

Ambrose Halder was clearly determined to have him as his house guest, and Tony Duchenne thought of the pleasant change it would be to have the use of a bathroom, and a bed where there would be no unwelcome night irritants. Acapulco had some inferior accommodation if you were not prepared to pay the earth.

They went out into the evening sunshine and down another series of steps on the other side of the villa; there was a stone-built garage set into the slope at the bottom where the ground levelled out. A young man in a striped sweat shirt and jeans was polishing a car, a large dark red Renault.

'This is Ernesto, Mr Duchenne,' said Halder. 'He will take you where you wish to go. He is a very careful driver, is that not the truth, Ernesto?'

Ernesto's face broke into a smile, flashing white teeth on display. He was several shades darker than Halder; high-shouldered and slim, in his early twenties.

'Yassuh,' he said happily. He took down a denim jacket that hung on the wall of the garage, and opened the passenger's door.

They drove sedately past the gates through which Halder had taken Tony and the lieutenant, and the minute they were out of sight of the villa, Ernesto put his foot down, swinging round the curves with much abandon, and giving the Renault's excellent suspension a merciless pounding on the bumpy surface of the track. If Ernesto was a sample of a careful driver by local stand-ards, Tony Duchenne was glad he wasn't being driven by a careless one.

Ernesto didn't do any talking, which sur-prised Tony, and he couldn't think of a tactful way of bringing up the matter of Ambrose Halder and what manner of man his employees thought he was. He wondered also if the shooting business was known about among the menials; the visit of the police lieutenant would surely have been known about and gossiped about.

Ernesto just banged that nice car along gleefully, and when they got in among the evening traffic he made imperious noises with his hooter at anybody, motorist or pedestrian, who challenged his right of way. He evidently enjoyed being behind a wheel, and treated the Renault as a weapon to be used competitively.

Tony Duchenne found it hard on his nerves; they had near-misses, and Ernesto was justifiably sworn at by fellow-travellers after some of his outrageous manoeuvres, but they reached the *pension* where Tony had been lodging and the car hadn't been scratched, which was a small miracle.

Tony had paid for a week in advance, and he still had three days to go, but the owner of the *pension* pointed out that there couldn't be any refund because of the lack of the requisite notice. Tony packed his bag in a matter of minutes, and went down to Ernesto, who was waiting in the car.

On the return journey he made a plea for a

less spectacular progress, and Ernesto, a little puzzled at first at what he took to be his passenger's craziness, finally got the message, and reduced speed, just a little, although it plainly grieved him, especially when other drivers overtook him. And hooted at him.

Before they were back at the villa Tony had got its name: the *Villa Hermosa*, the Beautiful Villa.

Beautiful was not quite the word for it, he reflected. Its position was its real feature, and its remoteness. It was not a place where the host would have jolly parties. Acapulco was one of the fun spots in the sun, catering to the shoals of rich idlers who jetted in from the States.

The *Villa Hermosa* was stuck up there on its rock all by itself. And that was where Ambrose Halder had chosen to live. Clearly a man of some substance, look at how respectful that young police officer had become as soon as he saw Halder on the pavement among those excited citizens.

Back at the villa, Halder had introduced him to Madame Clara, his housekeeper. She was about thirty, with auburn hair and a clear cool complexion that had not been exposed to much of the strong sunshine; she had a slender figure, and her smile was quite charming; an elegant woman, and not at all the kind of domestic worker Tony Duchenne had expected to find in that household, and he found himself speculating about the extent of her housekeeping duties. So far there had been no mention of a Mrs Halder.

She showed him up to his room; his solitary case had already been brought up; travelling light was going to have its drawbacks, and he thought his wardrobe was going to be a little limited for the *Villa Hermosa*.

Madame Clara understood his position. She smiled.

'We are informal here, Mr Duchenne. We dine late or early, whichever suits Senor Halder, so come down when you wish, and if there is anything you need the bell will bring me. I hope you will enjoy your stay with us, the Senor sees too few visitors, and you will be good for him.'

With another charming smile she took herself off, leaving Tony to inspect his surroundings. There was a modern divan bed, and all the furnishings of the room were bright and cheerful, in sharp contrast to the room below. There was a bathroom attached and a shower stall – a distinct luxury after the places he had been stopping at during his wanderings across Mexico.

He unpacked a clean shirt that was almost presentable, and some slacks that came out of his bag with creases in the right places. He took a long shower, finishing with the cold spray bouncing on his body, very invigorating.

His window looked away inland, with the flower beds and the steps down the slope, and because of the uneven ground his view was strictly limited; he could just see the roof of the garage and some other small buildings that had been hidden by the jutting rocks. Down by the gate he noticed three men, and he recognised one of them as Ernesto; the other two looked older men, and both of them carried rifles, not sporting guns, but rifles.

There was some arm waving by one of the men, like a platoon commander giving tactical instructions to the troops; then the group split up, and Tony lost sight of them. Presently he saw one of them settling himself on a rocky shelf from which he would have a clear view of the approach to the villa by road. He was obviously on sentry duty, squatting with his rifle resting across his thighs, very alert and not smoking.

The light was fading, and the ground was so uneven that it was impossible to get much of a view. Tony wondered how many men there were down there, guarding the villa.

The cause of it all had to be the shooting down in the town, the shooting that Ambrose Halder had dismissed so casually as just a political matter and thus just not worth bothering about. Clearly politics were taken seriously in these parts. Tony Duchenne smoked a cigarette and stood looking out over the darkening scene. It looked peaceful. What would happen if an unwelcome visitor came up that twisty drive?

Nobody arrived to oblige him, and now it was too dim to pick out any kind of detail.

Ambrose Halder had changed into a black velvet jacket with silver piping, a white frilly shirt, and dark trousers. With his spare and upright figure and dark saturnine face he looked the part, the grandee who was used to gracious living, and that would not include being flat on his belly on the pavement with bullets whistling about.

They went into a long glass-fronted portico that ran along part of the seaward side of the villa. There were hanging plants and the traditional checked tiles and some wicker lounging chairs, and delicate wrought-iron tables. The sea appeared closer than ever; there was a low wall, and then nothing, just a sheer drop to the water.

'We dine in half an hour, if that will suit you, Mr Duchenne,' said Halder. 'We have time for an aperitif. May I recommend to you the amontillado?'

Tony couldn't pretend to be a connoisseur of sherry, but he had to agree with his host that this was indeed a memorable and fine wine, dry enough to sharpen the palate; it was also considerably superior to anything Teresa had in her cellar in the hotel in Jamaica, and Teresa had fancied she knew something about wine.

'Your continued good health,' said Halder, lifting his glass. 'Let us sit and become better acquainted before Madame announces dinner. You have questions you wish to ask me.'

'One or two,' said Tony.

'Perhaps first of all you will tell me something about yourself,' said Halder.

'What would you like to know? I'm a French-Canadian. I have no ties. So I travel. And I'm here.'

Halder smiled and teased his little goatee beard between his finger and thumb. 'An admirable summary. It provokes the imagination. Would you care to elaborate, or am I being tiresome?'

Tony Duchenne reflected on what to leave out. It seemed he had to humour the old boy. So he started.

4

He gave a very carefully edited version of the story of his life. He made no reference to the fact that at one time he had been thought a suitable candidate for the Church, and he naturally omitted all details about his marital fiasco in Jamaica. He gave, he thought, a convincing portrait of himself as a foot-loose wanderer; not exactly a drop-out, but a young man with his own ideas and his own set of values, and not at all ready to accept the conventions that make for a respectable member of society.

'You have no profession?' said Halder mildly. 'You have been well educated, don't you feel you are wasting your life?'

'So far I haven't found anything I want to do sufficiently badly to devote myself to it,' said Tony. 'Perhaps I'm at heart just a drifter.'

'At your age,' said Halder, 'a measure of rebellion is expected from an intelligent man, it is the mark of an inquiring mind.'

'Nice of you to put it like that,' said Tony.

'I am expected to toe the line when I get older, I've heard that before. I just don't like much of what I've seen. Here and there.'

'Reality has a habit of intruding,' said Halder. 'One's ideals become a little tarnished as time passes. One has to compromise. It is a painful process, but inevitable for most of us, I fear.'

'I'm in no hurry,' said Tony.

'May I bore you with a little reminiscence?' said Halder. 'When the civil war in Spain was at its worst, I was a medical student at a London hospital. I was going to be a great surgeon. I have Spanish blood in my veins, as you will have gathered, and my family has always taken pride in its connections and lineage, although we have not lived in Spain for many generations. I abandoned my studies and went to Spain to offer my services, not as a combatant, but to help with the wounded. That might seem of no great importance, young men from many countries joined in the fighting on both sides, and Hitler and Mussolini sent men and tanks and aircraft to get war experience on Franco's side. That is now old history. I joined the International Brigade, I supported the government that lost in the end. When the collapse happened I got over the border into France with the other refugees. We were bitter and disillusioned, most of us, the losers. I managed to avoid being sent to an internment camp – I was still active enough, although my health had suffered. The real damage was what had been done to my spirit – I could never be the same man again afterwards.'

'I've never been in a war,' said Tony. 'I don't regret it. They always seem to me like museum pieces, stupid and pathetic, and criminal. There's no glory in it, not any more. So you survived and came back home?'

'Not as a hero,' said Halder. 'I had seen the worst and the best of what humanity can do. It was futile, all for nothing in the end. And I was in great disgrace with my family. To the day he died, my grandfather – a man I had loved and admired all my life – did not speak to me again except through a third person. If I entered a room he would get up and leave.'

'That's a bit harsh,' said Tony. 'Why?'

'By supporting the International brigade I had smirched the family honour. I was no better than a Communist, and to my grandfather they were anathema and beyond redemption. I was an atheist, I had sided with those who set fire to churches and murdered priests and ravaged nuns. God's hand had been against us, so we had lost. It was a bad time for me, but I lived through it.'

'Families can be pretty fierce, I know that from experience,' said Tony. 'They expect a lot. They always know best, and if you don't conform you're a renegade and a disgrace. What about your medical career?'

'There was none,' said Halder. 'I didn't go back to the hospital. Other commitments intervened. I became involved in other concerns.'

'Reality intruded itself,' said Tony. 'I am quoting your own words. From what I see, you've been prosperous. Those commitments must have paid off.'

'The Halders have been wealthy for a very long time,' said Ambrose Halder. 'Have you ever heard of Sansovino, Mr Duchenne?'

'I think so,' said Tony. 'Isn't it one of those banana republics where they're always having revolutions and so on? I must have heard of it somewhere.'

'It is true we do grow some bananas,' said Halder. 'But revolutions are not exactly a commonplace with us, in spite of the popular theory.'

'You mean you come from there?' said

Tony. 'That was clumsy and stupid of me–'

Ambrose Halder smiled. 'Please, there is no need to apologise. Sansovino is a small island, of no significance to the rest of the world. It has a beautiful climate and magnificent beaches; they have always been there, and we who lived on the island took our natural advantages for granted; life was not difficult – the sun shone and the crops grew without too much effort on our part.'

Tony Duchenne smiled to himself as he thought of Ambrose Halder working in a field under a blazing sun.

'I take it that your family were landowners?' he said.

'We were,' said Halder. 'It is true to say that we were the one important family on the island. We ran it. We provided employment, we built schools and a hospital, without us nothing would have been done for the general welfare of the island. It was old-fashioned paternalism, Mr Duchenne, but we took our obligations seriously. The islanders are a very mixed race, more so than in most of the islands, peasants, born field hands and fishermen; superstitious to a degree, and only nominally Christian. There was an Island Council, over which we presided – I was the last of my family to perform that function.'

Madame Clara appeared in the doorway and announced that dinner was served. She wore a black dress, with thin straps that left her fine shoulders bare, and it was cut so low at the back that her breasts had to be self-supporting; she wore no jewellery, only a small watch. As he followed her across into the dining-room Tony Duchenne thought he had seldom seen a woman with a more seductive movement, and from the exotic trail of perfume she left behind her he couldn't see her slaving over a hot stove in any kitchen. This was a lady who was surely geared for something very different, and that thought had him speculating about his host and his possible relationship with Madame Clara. Ambrose Halder was spry enough and fit enough.

Tony thought he could guess the end of Halder's story – he had been exiled from Sansovino, and he was sitting his time out at the *Villa Hermosa*.

They dined at a long black refectory table that could seat a dozen in comfort; just the three of them, and Madame Clara sat opposite Tony; the cutlery was heavy embossed silver, and the meal was served with some ceremony by menservants, deftly and in grave silence; coloured lads, looking like Ernesto.

The food was the best Tony Duchenne had eaten for some months, with some noteworthy wines.

Madame Clara did most of the talking. She knew London. She had been a pupil at an exclusive convent school in Surrey, and she had retained an enthusiastic interest in the Royal Family, particularly in the female members, and their social activities, and Tony had to confess that even after three years as a student in London he had never taken the trip to Windsor to gawp at the castle.

He had frequently been driven past Buckingham Palace without becoming ecstatic, and he didn't think he would cross the street to get a glimpse of Prince Charles or Prince Philip.

Madame Clara said she thought he was teasing her, but Ambrose Halder said, 'Mr Duchenne is a French-Canadian. He believes in a *Quebec Libre,* as did the late General de Gaulle. Am I right, Mr Duchenne?'

'You could be,' said Tony. 'I don't feel I have to look on England as my mother country, and plenty of Canadians think as I do.'

'A citizen of the world,' said Halder quietly, smiling. 'It is not an original idea.'

'My mother was English,' said Madame Clara. 'I was married to an Englishman for a little while. He was very dreary unless he had been drinking, and then he was impossible, so I divorced him. Did you ever go to watch the tennis at Wimbledon, Mr Duchenne?'

'Several times,' he said.

'Believe it or not,' she said, 'we have a hard court here with a very good playing surface, levelled out of ground below the garage. I like to play in the early morning, when I can find a partner who is willing to get up that early. I am seldom able to coax Senor Halder to give me a game.'

'I am getting beyond it,' said Halder. 'I prefer to be a spectator.'

Madame Clara was looking at him. 'Do you play, Mr Duchenne?'

'Not recently,' said Tony. Tennis and swimming were the only sports he had ever taken seriously, and he considered himself well above average at both of them. He really couldn't imagine this auburn-haired lovely with the creamy skin darting around a tennis court to much effect.

She was smiling, and it was a challenge.

'All right,' he said. 'I'm a bit stiff in one leg, but if I can borrow some gear I'll give you a game.'

'Oh dear,' she said, 'I had forgotten about your leg. Do forgive me, Mr Duchenne, that was very stupid of me ... we will forget the whole silly business.'

'When I had two good legs,' he said, 'I never played against a girl without giving her two or three games a set and a beating, and I played some pretty useful girls here and there. I think I can still cope on a tennis court.'

'It was not a sensible idea,' she said. 'I feel you've been tricked into this unfairly.'

'Tomorrow?' said Tony. 'What time?'

She glanced at Halder interrogatively. 'Mr Duchenne is our guest,' said Halder dryly. 'If he wishes to punish himself by chasing after a little white ball at dawn we must accommodate him. I have never understood this obsession with competitive so-called sports; it seems to me that human energy can be better employed in quite other directions. However, I may present myself to congratulate the victor.'

'Would seven be too early for you, Mr Duchenne?' said Madame Clara. 'I will see that everything is ready for you; we have spare rackets and you should not be difficult to fit in the way of shorts and so on.'

'Size eight in shoes,' said Tony.

'It would be much simpler if we agreed to play chess,' said Ambrose Halder.

'Sorry,' said Tony. 'I tried it and I never got anywhere.'

'You must stay with us long enough for me to give you some tuition,' said Halder. 'I have done my best to interest Madame here; she plays a fair game of tennis, but in front of a chess board she becomes quite capricious ... and feminine.'

'Such gallantry.' The lady reached across and tapped the back of Halder's hand on the table; just a fleeting touch, but suggesting so much more, and the quick smile on her face was not altogether that of a paid housekeeper to her employer – and Tony Duchenne watched the pair of them with renewed interest.

She caught his eye, and she might have guessed what he was thinking. She said, 'If you change your mind about the tennis, Mr Duchenne, don't give it another thought – I can always get a practice game with Ernesto.'

'I'll be there,' he said.

'You mustn't feel you've been badgered into this,' she said.

'I don't,' he said.

'We will take coffee in my study,' said Halder. 'Mr Duchenne and I have matters to discuss.'

'Of course,' said Madame Clara, rising. 'Then I will say good-night to you, Mr Duchenne.'

'Good-night,' said Tony. 'We'll meet to-morrow morning.'

Smiling, she said, 'I look forward to it.' She nodded at Halder and left.

Halder took Tony along a short corridor. There was a door at the end, and it was locked, which Tony thought was a little odd since this was Halder's home.

'This is the only room in the house where I can be sure of not being interrupted,' said Halder, unlocking the door. 'Nobody comes in here except by invitation.'

It was a small room, stale with old cigar smoke; there was one long narrow window, set high up in the wall; there were shelves of books, a desk, some steel filing cabinets; there was a swivel chair at the desk, and one other armchair; on a table by the desk there was an elaborate radio set, much too elaborate for normal domestic use, the kind of set that would look right in the ship's radio shack.

'Do please sit,' said Halder, indicating the armchair.

There was a soft tap on the door. Halder opened it. One of the men-servants was there with a trolley – coffee, a decanter, and cigars. The service at the *Villa Hermosa* was speedy and efficient. Halder took charge of the trolley and the servant went off. Halder poured the coffee, offered brandy and a cigar, settled himself at the desk, and Tony Duchenne surmised that the rest of the evening had been leading up to this.

'Are you expecting a siege?' he said.

'A siege?' said Halder.

'I saw those men down there in the garden,' said Tony. 'They had guns.'

'You have good eyesight,' said Halder.

'You were telling me about Sansovino,' said Tony. 'I gather you were evicted.'

'I could put it another way,' said Halder, 'but the end product comes to much the same thing.'

'You're in exile. Since when?'

'A little less than two years.'

'A bloodless revolution?' said Tony.

'No,' said Halder. 'My wife and my only son died, amongst others.'

'I'm sorry,' said Tony.

'I survived,' said Halder bleakly. 'Perhaps

it would have been better if I had died with them. There was little fighting, it was quickly done, and it is my everlasting shame that I escaped.'

For a few moments Halder pulled on his cigar in silence, his face heavy with remembered sadness. He reached up to a switch on the wall by his desk, and the silence was broken by the soft hum of the air-conditioning plant taking over, and the room became appreciably fresher.

'It was a political take-over, with a little killing in the process. My wife and my son and two of my oldest and best friends were put against a wall; they were caught in my country house in the hills before I could do anything to save them. I was a sick man, Mr Duchenne – what a time for a man to be helpless and sick. I was smuggled out of the country by loyal supporters who chose exile with me rather than life under the rule of the new men. The murderers. They called themselves the People's Progressive Party.'

Ambrose Halder smiled. 'I should have been warned beforehand. I was aware of the unrest being fomented by some Council members, the angry speeches and the secret meetings and the political propaganda that was being spread around the island. I was accused of being reactionary, of standing in the way of the people's progress – even of amassing a private fortune out of the sweat of the poor. I was the worst kind of tyrant. The simple fact that Halder money had kept the island solvent for so many years was ignored. Aloysius Morane is now the man, and I doubt if the people of Sansovino are happier under him than they were when I presided – he and a handful of men like him have made the island into a miniature police state. In my time we had two small country prisons, and they seldom held more than a few drunks. I hear it is very different now.'

'Aren't there any of your supporters left in the island?' said Tony.

'There is nothing so sophisticated as an underground movement,' said Halder, 'but there are some who regret now what has been done – and they have good reason to regret it. If you are asking whether I ever hope to go back, I am unable to give you a straight answer – I am finding it difficult to get reliable information out of the island. The situation may be worse than I know. Morane has imposed a strict censorship in recent months.'

'So there is no Halder party?' said Tony. 'You're in exile and you're isolated, and this evening somebody tried to kill you. Has anything like this happened before?'

'When I was living in Barranquilla,' said Halder. 'Soon after I moved into the house there was a small bomb thrown through a window. It killed three people who were in the room. But I was not one of them. Until this evening I did not think they had traced me here.'

'So you'd better be moving again,' said Tony. 'The next time they may be better shots.'

'And I may not have you to do my thinking for me,' said Halder. 'Is the brandy to your liking?'

'Excellent,' said Tony. 'Doesn't this present situation scare you a little?'

'There is something I want to do before I die. Aloysius Morane held the gun, he took it on himself to kill my wife and son, and my friends. He has been heard to boast of it, to make a joke of the way they died in the sunshine. That is something I hold in my heart, Mr Duchenne, and I wait only for the day when Morane faces a gun, and I will be the man to use it. How that may happen I have no idea, he is closely protected, and when he appears in public no stranger is allowed near him, all visitors are searched, and when he travels it is with an armed escort. As I told you, Sansovino is a police state.'

'You have a problem,' said Tony. 'What about the people who escaped with you?'

'There are few survivors,' said Halder. 'Some have lost heart and have gone their own way, and I cannot blame them. There is little to inspire in a fallen ruler who lives as I do, like a hermit on a cliff top.'

'You don't appear short of money,' said Tony, 'that must be some kind of consolation, if I may say so.'

'I did not arrive here as a penniless refugee,' said Halder. 'We Halders have always invested our money wisely, I have ample funds to draw on, here and elsewhere. I could move wherever I choose and live out the rest of my life in ease and comfort. I could go to America or Europe, somewhere where Morane would never reach me. But that is not what I intend to do. Am I making any sense to you? Night and day I think only of one man, and if I thought there was the slightest chance of meeting him face to face I would have gone to Sansovino long ago, and I would die happily if I could take him with me. The last of the men in whom I could place any real trust was Doctor

Almeida, a man of my own age, but with far more courage than I will ever have.'

Ambrose Halder swung his swivel chair backwards and forwards, slowly, as though he was alone in the room. He was a loser all round, Tony decided. Nursing his impotent obsession with revenge instead of accepting the inevitable.

'Doctor Luis Almeida,' Halder went on softly. 'It was through his ingenuity and resourcefulness that I was got out of the island when I was so stupid with weakness that I knew nothing of what was going on around me. Ten days ago he went of his own free will and secretly back to Sansovino; he was going to gather information and assess the position there. For months I have been unable to find out anything; I have been maintaining a Press-cutting service, covering the whole of the Caribbean, looking for references to Sansovino. I had that radio installed, and I spend hours here alone tuning in to every station I can locate and listening to their news broadcasts, hoping to hear something about Sansovino, something I can use. I hear nothing. And Luis Almeida has not returned. It cannot be coincidence that there was an attempt on my life this evening.'

'You think he told them where to find you?' said Tony.

'Never willingly,' said Halder. 'He will be dead by now. I pray he is – Aloysius Morane would not deal with a man like Luis Almeida in a civilised manner. There are ways of tricking and breaking even the bravest of men, and Morane is very well equipped to do just that. I should never have let Luis go; he was too well known by sight to escape discovery; but it was his own choice.'

'You don't think there's still a chance you may hear from him?' said Tony. 'Perhaps he's had to lie low.'

'No chance of that now,' said Halder. 'It has been too long; he would have got a message back to me if he found himself unable to travel, I would have heard something – he was not a man to be easily defeated. It does not make a very lively or entertaining story, does it, Mr Duchenne? You have been very good to listen to me … an old man with his personal tragedies and disasters, I fear I have wearied you.'

'Not at all,' said Tony. 'I only wish I could suggest something that might help.'

'Allow me the pleasure of your company,' said Halder. 'Please don't feel you must go too soon. The *Villa Hermosa* can do with a little cheering up. I regret we have no swimming pool, it was just not feasible to build one up here; we have to pump our own water and generate our own power. As you will have noticed, we have no neighbours. It has been for me an ideal location.'

'Those men in that car must have been aware of your movements,' said Tony. 'They must have been trailing you.'

'Not a pleasant thought,' said Halder. 'I must alter my habits.'

'Or move out pretty smartly,' said Tony. 'I think that's what I'd do.'

'I am considering it,' said Halder. 'I expect tomorrow there will be a polite visit from an important police officer. Shooting in the streets of Acapulco is not something to be encouraged, it creates a bad impression on the visitors. My departure from Barranquilla was officially suggested after the bomb incident, although I would have left in any case. The same may well happen here. Until then I will take what precautions I can.'

He got to his feet, and there was nothing in his manner that indicated he was a man who stood a very good chance of not living much longer.

He held out his hand. 'I have talked enough. Sleep well, Mr Duchenne.'

'Thank you, I always do,' said Tony, as they walked to the door.

'The benefit of a clear conscience and a healthy constitution,' said Halder, smiling.

'When I was a student in London, not so long ago,' said Tony, 'I often saw a notice stuck up over the bar in some of the pubs – *Why worry? It may not happen.* Not a bad piece of advice.'

Ambrose Halder laughed quietly and saw him out. The British were a nation of survivors. They had had long practice at it.

Up in his room Tony found that some thoughtful soul had noticed his preference for 'Johnny Walker' – there was a bottle of it on his bedside table, with a glass and soda water. While he had been listening to Ambrose Halder downstairs he had done a little justice to the brandy, which was not his favourite drink. So he poured himself a whisky and sat by the window with the light out.

Over the high ground there was the reflected glow of the lights from the town, but not a flicker of light from anywhere nearby. It was a starlit night, and the broken ground was full of strange shadows among the rocks and crevices, and he wondered if Halder's armed men were enjoying their vigil down there. It was, he thought, most unlikely that the assassins who had made such a mess of things from a moving car would try a frontal assault on the villa. They would wait for an easier opportunity, and Ambrose Halder would have to make sure they didn't get it.

What a strange character Halder was. There was plenty in him worth admiring. He had guts, and he was ready to die if he could achieve his purpose, and Aloysius Morane would know that as well. There was grief and guilt in the old man, and the guilt was because he had not been there to die with his wife and his son and his friends.

Tony tried to recall reading about the coup in Sansovino, but he couldn't. Two years ago he had been in London, and, as Halder had put it, Sansovino was of little interest to the rest of the world. It wouldn't have made a stir in the world's news. Just another island revolution, with the unlucky losers stuck up against a wall and shot. Except for Ambrose Halder, the lost leader, with those ample funds so wisely invested abroad against such a day of disaster. A commonplace story. Except also that by the purest mischance that unheroic figure, Tony Duchenne, had been on hand to save the gentleman from a violent death, and now enjoyed his abundant hospitality.

Sipping his whisky, Tony found himself in a sober and reflective mood. Halder insisted on showing his gratitude. As the lady remarked, if rape is inevitable, lie back and enjoy it. If Ambrose Halder wanted to make a fuss over him, there was no harm in being amenable – so long as he wasn't going to be expected to dodge any more bullets.

She was in bed when he came in quietly without knocking, in a long dark blue dressing-gown, tightly belted so that it made him appear taller and leaner than ever.

She had been reading, a novel by an English writer, Iris Murdoch. The pillows were heaped at her back, her auburn hair was loose and deeply shining over the pillows. She wore pale green pyjamas, no sleeves to the jacket, and the bedside light gleamed on her rounded arms and shoulders. She looked beautiful, her face serene and her hooded eyes welcoming his arrival.

'Well?' she said, putting her book down and preparing to listen like a dutiful spouse even though it was now midnight. 'How did it go with our visitor?'

Halder settled himself in a wicker-work

chair by the bed, primly folding the skirt of his dressing-gown over his knees.

'An interesting young man,' he said. 'Quite intelligent. He chooses to conceal his background, but he is a good listener.'

'How much did you tell him?' Madame Clara adjusted the pillows at her back.

Her firm breasts moved under the thin jacket as she shifted her position, but Halder was looking across the room to the curtained windows.

'I told him enough,' he said. 'I aroused his sympathy, I think, and his interest. He will not be leaving us too soon, I hope. A French-Canadian, well educated, travelling without too much money, I fancy. What did you think of him?'

'He has spirit,' she said, 'and independence. I think there might be a lot in him worth discovering.'

Halder shifted his gaze back to her. 'He is aware of you.'

'Naturally,' she said. 'I would feel insulted if he saw me only as part of your furniture. Am I to encourage him? It would not be difficult.'

'I leave that to your discretion,' he said. 'You are a clever woman as well as being beautiful.'

'That is no kind of an answer.' Her voice had sharpened. 'You think you may have a use for him?'

'Possibly. He clearly has courage, and he is not a fool.'

'He is no fool at all,' she said. 'He will have guessed at our relationship.'

'He is a young man,' said Halder, 'and young men are not too critical of a beautiful woman, she must be allowed her little frailties, my dear one – it adds a spice to the romantic quest.'

She laughed quietly, and there was little amusement in it. 'You mean it proves that I'm accessible,' she said. 'So much for romance.'

He reached across the bed and took one of her hands in both of his. 'You are tired,' he said softly. 'You should be sleeping.'

'I will not behave like a whore, even for you,' she said.

'We are quarrelling too often lately,' he said. 'You are tired of being here with me; you have given me over a year of your life, and now I think you see no future in it for you. Am I right?'

'I see nothing for either of us – except that one day Morane's men will catch you and kill you … and what do you think that will do to me?'

'No,' he said firmly. 'It will not be like that. We both need to be away from here.' He stroked her arm with the tips of his fingers, slowly and gently. 'This has become no better than a prison. It is no life for you. You deserve more than this after the happiness you have given me.'

'If you could put Morane out of your mind,' she said, 'then we could go away and live – really live.'

'We will do that,' he said. 'There is just one more chance I want to try, if I can persuade this young man.'

'I don't think I want to hear about that now,' she said. 'I will help you with him all I can – if that is the only way I can have you to myself.'

'You are too good to me,' he said.

'And now you are going back to your own bed?' she said. 'I am forgetting what it is like to have you beside me – you have been too occupied with other matters, sitting down there alone in your study until late in the night, brooding … it is not good for you. Tomorrow I will act the obedient servant, and if this Mr Duchenne reacts the way I know he will, what then?'

'Keep him interested.'

She gave him a sidelong glance. 'I might begin even to enjoy it.'

'Then you will make your act all the more convincing.'

'We tread dangerous ground,' she said softly.

Very deftly he reached across the bed and slipped her jacket up over her head, and she made no demur, just settled herself deeper into the pillows. When he kissed her breasts she cradled his head in her hands, an expression of quiet contentment on her face. He was in no hurry and he knew what pleased her most. As a lover, he was always considerate, and very expert. And tonight was no exception, when he slid out of his dressing-gown in one sinuous movement without breaking contact, and she flung her arms wide in the ecstasy of it. There was nothing else that mattered.

5

He was awake in plenty of time, and he felt sharp and alert; he had taken a quick shower when a cheerful manservant arrived with a complete set of tennis kit, all either new or freshly laundered; the white shorts were a little generous around the middle, but they were wearable enough; there was a white singlet, and size eight shoes.

'Madame has the coffee downstairs, sah,' said the servant. 'She has the rackets for you to choose.'

'The resources of the *Villa Hermosa* are infinite,' said Tony.

'Sah?'

Tony shooed him out and changed. He had been intending to shave off his beard, since it had served its purpose, but there wasn't time for that now.

She was waiting in the hall, and she was, he decided, a sight well worth getting up early to see. She had tight white shorts that instantly teased the imagination – the smooth firm-fleshed legs of a show-girl and a neat rear. She wore a white blouse and a cream jersey knotted loosely by the sleeves around her neck, and her hair was tied neatly back with a white ribbon. She looked as fresh as the morning.

There were rackets on the table and a tray with coffee. She poured for him and said, 'I still think it's a dreadful shame getting you up so early on your first morning with us.'

'I wouldn't have it otherwise,' he said, 'and I kid you not.'

While he sipped his coffee – it was strong and black – she walked over to the glass-fronted door and stood gazing out. The sun was up and bright, but not yet strong, and she made a very attractive picture.

'You slept well, Mr Duchenne?' she called over her shoulder.'

'Very well, thank you,' he said. 'Since you are about to take the hide off me at tennis, don't you think Mr Duchenne is a trifle formal?'

She turned and gave him a brilliant smile. 'That sounds very sensible, Tony. I'm afraid you'll be much too good for me.'

'Don't put any money on it, Clara.'

They went out into the clear sunshine, down some wide shallow steps that zig-zagged across the garden and then down until the villa was out of sight beyond the garage building. The tennis court had been levelled out on the only reasonably flat piece of ground in the area; it was enclosed on all sides by a jagged wall of rocks, and when the sun was high it would be little better than an oven. Somebody had spent time and plenty of money in scooping out a space large enough.

'It was here when we arrived,' Clara said. 'We had it tidied up – it was in a pretty derelict state, but it plays fairly well now, unless it's been raining.'

They spent a few minutes knocking up, and he could see that she had received some sound coaching; her footwork was right, and she didn't hurry her shots.

When they started playing he found he had to move around to some purpose; her game was steady, and those attractive legs covered the court very effectively, and she asked for no mercy. He took the first set six-four, and he had to work for it.

He was happy to rest before they changed over, and he noted that she was showing nothing in her face for all the chasing about he'd been making her do on the base-line. No shiny nose. No sweat. Just those breasts heaving under her blouse. She was undeniably decorative, and she was fitter than he imagined. Quite a surprise as a house-keeper in a remote villa perched on the rocks where social visitors were clearly not expected or encouraged.

'Before you had that trouble with your leg,' she said, 'you would have been right out of my class. What happened, Tony?'

'A bullet,' he said. 'I was in the wrong place at the wrong time. Shall we try another set?'

He pressed her a little harder and more persistently this time, angling his service so that she had to shift quickly to take it, and she did pretty well for a while. Her game didn't break up even when she began to trail well behind.

At four-two in his favour he eased up; he was having some twinges with his leg, and she went in for some crafty lobs that had him scurrying about, not too agilely. At five-all she said she'd had enough, and he gave her no argument. Honour had been satisfied.

As they climbed up to the villa she said, 'One day I want to hear about that bullet.'

'A sordid little episode,' he said.

'That makes it all the more interesting,' she said. 'Breakfast will be whenever you're ready.'

They had breakfast in a pleasant, sunny room which was a distinct improvement on the monastic room where they'd had dinner the night before. There was a view of the sea which was placid and sparkling with the sun.

There were just the two of them. She had changed into white slacks and a white and green striped jersey and she explained that Ambrose Halder seldom took breakfast.

'I have been commissioned to look after you,' she said brightly. 'Ambrose expects to be busy part of the time talking to a police officer or one of the important ones from the town, about that dreadful business last night. But that is no reason for us to be confined to the villa ... have you ever done any sailing, Tony?'

'Very little,' he said.

'We have a dinghy we keep down on the coast,' she said. 'We might try a sail, would that amuse you?'

'I am willing and able to heave on a rope, under your instruction,' he said, 'but I am no mariner.'

'With the sea like this,' she said, indicating the shining ocean below their window, 'I don't fancy there will be any trouble.'

'One favour,' he said, 'I wouldn't want to

be driven anywhere by Ernesto, I couldn't stand a repeat of yesterday's hazards.'

She laughed and promised they would drive themselves. 'I might put up a picnic lunch,' she said, 'and there's a place where we can swim, if we feel energetic.'

'An interesting programme,' he said. She was surely going out of her way to occupy him, and he didn't imagine it was going to prove any hardship from where he sat – it was a long time since he had enjoyed the company of an attractive woman.

'You won't be bored?' she said. 'I seem to be dragging you into all sorts of activities – you may prefer just to laze here in the sun? Do say.'

'Let's play truant,' he said. 'I am at your disposal. And willingly.'

'Good,' she said, getting up. 'I have a few things to see to, and then we can be off.'

They used the red Renault again, and Tony noticed a blue sports job in the garage – smart but too low-slung for the poor roads in their immediate area. They had a hamper on the back seat, and the lady drove, with economy and precision, just as she had played her game of tennis. On the way out a lounging figure waved to them from the scanty shelter of an outcrop of rock; if he had a gun he kept it out of sight.

'Halder doesn't think it might be dangerous for you to go out like this?' said Tony.

'I have a gun,' she said, 'and I am a good shot. Also, I am not alone, am I?'

Tony digested the information, and began to look out for other vehicles on the road. He appeared to have been elected as a bodyguard, whether he liked it or not. An intimidating prospect all round.

'There is nothing to worry about,' she said. 'It is not me that Morane is after. I am not that important.'

'Perhaps you'd better let me have the gun,' he said.

She had brought a large wicker bag, it sat on the floor of the car at her feet, between them.

'In there,' she said. 'Under the bathing things. Leave it there, then we can both reach it – do you shoot well, Tony?'

'I duck a lot better,' he said. And left the gun where it was. They were driving south, on a good coast road; there was plenty of traffic, all of it moving fast, and at no time did another car do anything suspicious – like slowing alongside and pushing them off the road. So Tony began to relax. The holiday spirit was abroad, almost.

'Will you be sorry to leave the villa?' he said.

She shrugged. 'In a way. It has been quiet and peaceful there, and I have been happy.'

'Have you made any friends around here?'

'A few. We have entertained very little.'

'How did you come to meet Ambrose Halder?' he said. 'You weren't in Sansovino, were you?'

'No,' she said. 'I have never been there. I met him in Mexico City. He was looking for a housekeeper, and I needed a job. I have been with him ever since.'

'An interesting man,' said Tony.

She made no reply. She was not prepared to discuss Halder with Tony Duchenne.

After they had covered some miles at a fair speed, she turned off the main coast highway on to a road that led down between high cliffs covered in dark green and brown scrub. And now they began to feel the real power of the sun. It was mid-morning, and not a cloud in the sky. There were fleeting glimpses of patches of the sea as the road twisted back on itself, and Clara was driving with extra care because the bends were so sharp and frequent.

She braked when they came to a junction.

There was a gate across the side road, and a sign: *Marina Paradiso*. Tony got out and opened the gate and she drove in. Half a mile down they were in sight of the sea, and the crowded spread of the marina with the neat lines of craft tied up.

There was a club house with a veranda and some striped deck chairs on the grass where a few young children were playing; there was plenty of colour and activity, with the bright hulls of the dinghies and the brown and white and blue sails of the ones already sailing out beyond the arm of the marina. There were some expensive cars in the parking space under the cliffs behind the club house.

There was a pleasant family atmosphere, upper-income bracket family, and at that hour in the morning only the leisured or the holiday-makers would be free to go sailing.

As they humped their gear along the wooden boardwalk, Tony noticed that some of the men who were doing their traditional messing about in boats gave Clara a sort of greeting – a wave or a salute, but the younger women were not aware of her presence, and Tony wondered if that was because she was so much more attractive than any of them. They were all tanned as brown as field hands, and she had preserved that creamy flawless complexion, which must make her a serious menace socially.

If she was conscious of the ostracism she gave no sign of it. She had produced a peaked cap, and on her it didn't look like fancy dress; it just looked the sensible thing to wear on a small boat.

'Here she is,' she said, halting by a red-hulled dinghy.

'It doesn't look very big,' said Tony cautiously.

'It's a Fireball, specially imported from England,' she said. 'It doesn't look fancy, but it can outsail most of the things around here. It's quite safe if you don't do anything silly in a wind.'

'They're all watching us,' said Tony, 'so you'd better tell me what to do. I hear these seafaring types are highly critical and I would hate to have them hooting at us.'

Together they got the sails set and made a creditable departure without any outrageous mishaps. Clara had the helm and Tony disposed himself as much out of the way as he could, which was not all that simple since a Fireball is designed for racing and not a lounging passenger.

'There is so little wind that we will not

have to put you on the trapeze,' she said. 'This is not good sailing weather.'

'If you mean I won't have to lean out over the angry sea on the flimsy grating thing I'm very happy,' said Tony. 'Does Ambrose sail?'

'He is excellent,' she said shortly. She was scanning the sea ahead of them, looking for a ripple on the surface that would indicate a breeze. 'At the last club regatta we won five races out of seven.'

The water poppled busily along the sleek sides of the dinghy; a few inquisitive gulls swept down, found nothing to salvage in their slow wake and wheeled away; the other dinghies that had put out before them were now widely scattered, and they appeared to have the wide expanse of the ocean to themselves; behind them the receding cliffs and the club house and the marina were still clear in outline.

'Not very exciting, I'm afraid,' she said.

'Are we aiming for anywhere in particular?' he asked.

'There's a small island,' she said. 'It's mostly rock, but we can tie up and there's a good place to swim. At this rate it will take us at least a couple of hours.'

'I can't think of a better way of passing a sunny morning,' he said. 'Don't you get any

105

social life at the sailing club?'

'They sent us invitations at first,' she said. 'We did not accept them. They have dances and cocktail parties and beach barbecues, all the usual things. When we won those races Ambrose was a little concerned about the publicity, our pictures in the papers and so on; he thought it might be dangerous – we were hoping to live privately.'

'It didn't work, did it?' he said. 'It would have been safer if you had moved right away, America, Europe–'

'He wished to remain within reasonable reach of Sansovino, that was the only reason why we chose to live here as we have done.'

'It doesn't seem to have done much good,' he said.

'One can always hope,' she said.

'Vengeance is mine, saith the Lord. I will repay.'

'You do not understand,' she said. 'I fancy the breeze has freshened, so we might try the spinnaker.'

She gave him the helm and told him what to look out for and what not to do. Very deftly she got the striped spinnaker up and almost immediately it began to fill and the dinghy heeled slightly and quickened through the water. It was quite exhilarating.

She gave him some elementary lessons on the technique of using the trapeze, and in spite of his previous reluctance to get involved he was pleased when she eventually told him that he had the makings of a good crew-man.

They came up with the island, a heap of jagged rocks that looked unfriendly at first glance, but she steered them round until they were gliding into a tiny inlet made by the fissure in the rocks where there was a clear white sandy bottom that shelved gently and made it possible for the dinghy to be tied up neatly to a finger of rock. The whole jagged area was no bigger than a tennis court, thick with bird droppings and green and brown with weed. She showed him the one shady spot, under an overhang of rock, and there they dumped their hamper.

'I've never seen anybody else here,' she said. 'I believe they call it the *Devil's Tooth*, in bad weather it's a dangerous hazard and none of the local sailors ever come near it. I've come here on my own several times. It's so remote it fascinates me, when I'm in the mood.'

She unpacked the hamper. There was salad and cold chicken and fruit and a chilled white wine and even some cans of beer, and a large Thermos of coffee; it was no sketchy meal. Madame Clara had done her house-keeping more than adequately.

'This is very pleasant,' he said lazily. 'Miles from anywhere.'

'I'm glad you're not bored,' she said. 'Are you married, Tony?'

'Unsuccessfully,' he said. 'Mostly my fault.'

'You don't want to talk about it?' she said.

'There's no point,' he said. 'I left her. I didn't fit in with her arrangements. She's all right financially, much better off than I am. I expect she will divorce me for desertion.'

'So what brought you to Mexico?'

'In flight from the broken romance.'

She laughed.

'That's the honest truth,' he said.

'You're not being serious with me,' she said, 'and you're quite right, I'm just prying.'

'A thought occurs to me,' he said. 'If Ambrose Halder is having an interview with the police about that shooting business, shouldn't I be there? I was involved.'

'Indeed you were,' she said, 'and very effectively. But Ambrose will manage. No-body was hurt, and Ambrose has had much experience in handling officials, and they will respect his wishes for no publicity.'

'That suits me,' said Tony, privately very relieved. He was now travelling under his own name, and if Teresa had put out a general police call after him as her runaway and defaulting husband, the information might have reached the Mexican authorities, and he was not all that anxious to jog the memories of any police officers in Acapulco.

'It was a clumsy business,' he said.

'You are a modest man,' she said. 'Most men would expect to have a great fuss made of them if they had done what you did.'

'I am a devout coward,' he said. She laughed again, a very pleasant and friendly sound. 'When you leave Mexico, what then?'

'I haven't made up my mind,' he said.

'You can't go on wandering about.'

'Too true,' he said. 'I may even be compelled to look for some congenial and gainful employment.'

'Do you have anything in view, Tony?'

'Not a thing,' he said cheerfully. 'I depend solely on myself. I am a cautious optimist.'

'But you must have plenty of friends,' she said, 'and yet you seem happy to travel on your own.'

'I have friends, here and there,' he said. 'I don't live in a vacuum.'

'I'm sorry, I'm prying again.'

109

'Feel free,' he said. 'I don't mind.'

There were many less pleasant ways of passing time than sitting alone with an attractive woman and letting her ask personal questions. There was one topic he wasn't going to be drawn on, and that was his disastrous and short-lived marriage.

If she wanted to talk about his girl friends, he thought he had more than enough ammunition to satisfy her. And then he might even put a few pertinent questions himself, such as about her and Ambrose Halder. A woman as attractive as she was wouldn't have accepted the isolated life of the *Villa Hermosa* unless there were compensations – perhaps she was in love with Halder.

Tiny ripples washed over the fine white sand at their feet; sea birds waited on nearby rocks for any scraps that might be tossed their way, and then squabbled noisily over the plunder; the dinghy sat mirrored in the water, slender red hull and mast, tugging gently at the painter; the smell of the sea was strong all round them.

'There must be some good fishing around here,' he said. 'The big ones – tarpon, marlin, barracuda.'

'And sharks,' she said, 'but you couldn't

do that kind of fishing from a dinghy like ours, you'd need a cruiser with an engine and the right gear. I went out once, but it didn't appeal to me. My sympathies were with the fish and I was rather glad when they got away – they fought so hard for freedom. But if you'd really like a fishing trip Ambrose could have it arranged.'

'But you wouldn't come with me?' he said, and she smiled as she shook her head.

They had long finished their lunch, and out beyond their little spot of shade the sea sparkled in the afternoon sun; she had smoked just one cigarette, which she said was her allowance; she made no mention of returning to the mainland; she had rolled up the legs of her slacks and he noticed her fine slender feet, with the straight toes and the high insteps – many beautiful women had catastrophic feet; not this one. The afternoon slid silently along.

She lay with her head pillowed on one arm, and her eyes shut, and presently he thought she was asleep, so to sit there so close beside her seemed an intrusion. The front of her striped jersey had come loose from the top of her slacks and he knew she wore no brassiere.

He climbed out into the sun and sat up on top of the rocks, and the heat was like a smack over his back and shoulders. He tried a cigarette, but it tasted of nothing but scorched dried grass. He had to search about before he could find anywhere to squat among the bird droppings and jagged bits of rock, and the general smell was pretty high. He found a small ledge on the other side of the island where he could sit and dangle his feet in the water, which helped a little.

He could just make out a few sailing craft in the distance, and a cargo ship well down on the horizon, otherwise the sea was all his.

He wondered if she had ever brought another man to share that deserted lump of rock with her, and he wasn't thinking of Ambrose Halder. She said she had been there on her own, when she had been in the mood.

She was clearly no sunbathing addict, not with that nice pearly skin; you could fry yourself inside half an hour on the rocks; already his shoulders were beginning to prickle under his shirt, and he had a good tan to begin with.

Ambrose Halder had told her to amuse their heroic guest, and she was surely going to some trouble to do that. Tennis at the crack of dawn, and now this sea trip to a remote chunk of rock. What might the evening hold?

An enterprising and intriguing pair, the deposed autocrat and his lovely housekeeper.

When he climbed down she wasn't there. Her clothes had been tidily folded to one side, slacks and striped jersey and so on. The dinghy was still bobbing in the shallows, so she hadn't marooned him.

Then she appeared, picking her way along the rocks just clear of the water. Her swim suit was black, cut high on her thighs, a one-piece outfit that was absolutely right for the fine flowing lines of her figure, and far more sexy than any skimpy bikini would have been. She wore a white bathing cap. Her face was full of animation, and she flicked the shining drops of water from her arms and legs, smiling.

'There's a safe place along there for diving,' she said. 'Are you coming in, Tony? You'll find some trunks in the basket.'

He dug in the basket. He found towels and a pair of blue trunks. He also found the gun, wrapped in brown paper. He lifted it out and glanced at her.

'What a hell of a thing to bring on a

picnic,' he said.

'Why not forget it and join me?' she said calmly.

He put the gun back and started to undress, and if she still cared to watch he had nothing to be ashamed of. Standing there in that tight suit she was an overt challenge to anybody with any manhood left, and Tony just then was feeling far from impotent.

As he climbed into the trunks he glanced up. She hadn't moved. She was smiling.

'How very flattering, Tony,' she murmured, then turned and steadied herself and dived into the water very neatly. Using an economical long-distance crawl, she headed out to the open sea; a woman with many accomplishments – she played good tennis, she handled a racing dinghy with ease, and she swam like a champion.

And she was probably electrifying in bed. She was no muscle-bound female athlete.

She was floating on her back when he finally caught up with her.

Treading water, they faced each other. 'I've never kissed a girl out in the open sea before,' he said.

'No?' She let herself float towards him until he had both arms around her, and her legs came up and locked themselves behind him, and she was laughing when he kissed her.

'How was it?' she asked teasingly. 'Up to your expectations?'

'Damp but promising,' he said. 'You taste very good, and you feel marvellous.'

'What an eager young man you are,' she said. Her thighs had gripped him hard, and she was paddling her hands to keep them floating, leaning away from him. 'It is not possible for us to do any more out here, unless you wish to drown both of us.'

'What a way to die.' He had slipped one of her shoulders straps clear so that one breast was pushing at the water between them.

'I think not,' she said. She unclasped her legs, wriggled herself out of his arms and sank below him.

He trod water for a moment. So far and clearly no further. Yet. He went down after her and saw the faint flickering of her legs in the pale green water, swimming strongly away. He tried to chase her, but she had seen him and avoided him with little trouble. Then she slid up to the surface and set off for the rocks.

He had been too much of an opportunist. Perhaps he had read the signs wrongly and she had just been indulging in a little open-air frolic. But he was recalling what she had said – that it wouldn't be possible for them to do any more out there in the sea. That was a promise of sorts, wasn't it? He hadn't made love to a woman of any refinement for months and months. There had been just a few episodes while he was on the run from Teresa and Jamaica, but they had been most commercial and fairly squalid. It must be the Mexican sunshine and the sea air.

It would be stupid if he made a really wrong move, then he would have to pack his bag, and he felt he wasn't ready to do that yet. Life at the *Villa Hermosa* had possibilities, and perhaps he had been wrong about her and Halder, they were just employer and housekeeper. So she could be interested in Tony Duchenne. Why not? There would be other opportunities.

The sea was milky and buoyant; you could almost fall asleep while swimming, and there were no signs of any dangerous currents … or sharks?

She would know, and she had swum out this far on her own. He made the return trip at his leisure, and he was not surprised to find that she had changed back into her jersey and slacks. She was drying the ends of her hair. And there was nothing outraged in her voice when she said, 'I've poured the remainder of the coffee, Tony, then I think we ought to be starting back.'

He drank the coffee, watching her. An apology would be out of order, he thought. If she was happy to pretend nothing of any significance had happened out there on the water between them, that was all right, he wasn't going to remind her.

She was rubbing a thin cream over her arms and the points of her shoulders, and he offered to do the back of her neck, a gentlemanly gesture.

'Thank you,' she said, handing him the pot of cream, 'it stops me blistering in the sea breeze. I can never take a sun tan, unfortunately; you look beautifully brown.'

'My peasant ancestry,' he said, gently working the stuff into her smooth skin. 'Very gross and earthy. Are you in love with Ambrose Halder? I don't apologise for asking.'

'You think I could be?' she said. 'You think you should ask me that, Tony? Is it just curiosity?'

He went on massaging the cream in, and when he had finished he caught hold of her arms and made her stand with him.

'It's not curiosity,' he said. Her face had become serious, and almost imperceptibly

117

she had moved into his reach, and when he kissed her it was nothing like the kiss when they had been bobbing about in the water. She gave herself to it fully with a sudden abandon that was beyond his wildest imaginings. It was as though the contact of their bodies had electrified her. Her fingers scorched down his naked back and her mouth was fast on his until he felt he could stand no more of this without taking her then and there on the sand by the edge of the water, blindly and savagely.

'Tony, Tony,' she murmured, stroking his cheek, 'we are not being sensible–'

'Sensible? Who the hell wants to be sensible? I'm in love with you, can't you tell that? Can't you?'

'It is not possible,' she said. 'You know nothing of me–'

'I know all I need to know,' he said. 'You're beautiful and I love you ... so what are we going to do about it?'

He held her fastened in against him, all that wonderfully pliant body, and he could feel the shaking of her legs, and the instinctive thrust of her pelvis into him.

'You know what I want,' he said. 'And you want it.'

6

She was murmuring broken protests against his mouth, incoherent endearments while she clung to him desperately, and he could have taken her off her feet and down on to the sand, and all would have been wonderful and complete for both of them.

Then she put a hand up over his mouth. 'Tony … it is too soon for that – and I am not being fair to you–'

'Fair?' he said, 'this isn't a game.' His voice was harsher than he had intended. 'I'm not trying to seduce you – I want to make love to you because that's the best way I know to show you what you mean to me.'

'You will please be patient with me,' she said, pleading. 'You will not be angry if I ask you to stop now?'

'All right,' he said. He let her go. She wasn't playing hard to get. There had been no faking in the way she had reacted to his embrace and the way he had felt her yielding. There was colour under that smooth skin, and her eyes, grey-green, were wide and bright, and tender.

'I wasn't mistaken, was I?' he said. 'It was the same for you. I know it was.'

She held out both hands in a gesture of helpless surrender. 'We give ourselves away.'

'So why pretend?' he said.

'Now you are angry with me.'

'I'm not angry,' he said.

'I think you should get dressed now. It is time for us to go.'

'Can we come here again?' he asked.

'Perhaps.'

She turned away from him and paddled across to the dinghy as though she had remembered something she had to do that would put a safe distance between them. He dressed. He was disappointed. Any hot-blooded male would be. But he knew something real had begun between them. He had never been a womaniser, a chaser. His early upbringing had left him with too many inhibitions where sex was concerned. It had never seemed all that terrific to him.

With her it would be different. It was like being on the threshold of another new world.

Together they loaded their gear on to the dinghy, and before they pushed off she said, 'Was she very beautiful, the wife you left?'

'Well now,' he said, 'beautiful wouldn't be quite the word I would choose. She was personable, and she could be attractive when she took the trouble. She had a good head for business, which most women of her age don't have.' He reflected for a moment. Too much honesty was not required. 'She was normal and healthy.'

'You must have been in love with her,' she said.

'I thought I was,' he said carefully. 'Very soon we found we were boring each other to distraction. We were just not on the same wavelength. So I skipped. Not a very romantic ending. End of episode.'

'I don't think you are really a frivolous person,' she said. 'That is not how I see you.'

'I have hidden depths,' he said. 'Who hasn't? A life of quiet desperation.'

'You make yourself sound unhappy,' she said. 'That is very sad, Tony.'

'There is a cure,' he said.

They got the dinghy under way and out into the open sea. There was more of a sailing breeze now, and Tony was kept busy doing what she told him so as to take full advantage of the wind, which effectively limited their conversation. She sat at the helm, concentrating on their course, and he thought she looked lovely and radiant. He wanted to reach out and touch her. He had never known a woman with such an air of quiet serenity. Almost like a nun. And she was no nun.

They were returning faster than they had come out, and with a freshening breeze the Fireball was showing her paces in a lively fashion, which gave Tony plenty of practice on the trapeze. There were two other sailing craft in the distance, ahead of them and on the same course, reaching in for the shelter of the marina.

With a series of precise manoeuvres which demanded some acrobatic efforts from Tony, the Fireball overhauled the craft in front of her and juggled her way past and into an easy lead, leaving some glum faces behind.

'I liked that,' said Tony. 'You did that very smartly.'

'How not to win friends,' she said. 'They hate being beaten by a woman. I was showing off, Tony – not a bit necessary.'

'If I could handle a boat the way you do,' he said, 'I'd show off all right.'

'It takes two to make a crew,' she said, 'and you were no handicap.'

'That makes my day,' he said. 'I'd kiss you if they weren't all gawping at us from the club house.'

'And that would make their day,' she said dryly. 'The Mexican members suspect I am a scarlet woman, and the visitors are quite sure I am.'

'So we don't pop into the bar for a quick livener?' he said.

'It would not be a good thing,' she said.

They made the Fireball fast and did all the chores incidental to small-boat sailing; the crews they had given a sailing lesson to came past with their gear, and this time Tony was the focus of their attention. He was the inferior male who had let a woman have the helm, which was not right. No women's lib here.

He persuaded her to let him drive back. They had just come out past the white gates when he noticed a truck parked on the side of the road; two men in the cab, swarthy, wearing working overalls. The truck started up as they passed and followed them.

When the Renault put on speed so did the truck, and as he watched in his mirror Tony began to feel a growing uneasiness. It might be nothing, just a truck with a couple of local workmen who happened to be going their way. Two men with dark skins? The country was full of them. It was their country.

He accelerated. This was where he would be the dynamic man of action. Clara sat up straighter.

'I don't like the look of the truck behind us,' he said. 'I'll lose it.'

'I noticed it,' she said. She didn't sound at all nervous.

The truck fell behind for a little while, and then came surging up again. It was no ordinary workman's vehicle, and it was being driven with determination.

'Slow up and let it pass, Tony,' she said calmly, reaching down into her basket. 'Then we shall see.'

He slowed and eased to the side of the road and waved the truck on. And he was not feeling altogether happy, because now she had that little automatic in her lap.

The truck came up alongside. The driver shouted something and flapped his hand to them to stop, and when Tony ignored the signal the truck swung in and there was a bump and a sound of metal crumpling, and the Renault was being forced off the road. There was no room to spare and the truck had angled itself so that Tony had to stop or hit it or run against the rocks on the side. So he stopped. And swore.

The driver of the truck and his mate got

out and the driver had a gun that he held against his leg. He was big, with a leather belt around his middle. He grinned and beckoned to Clara with the gun.

'We want you, lady. Don't let that feller of yours give us no bother now.'

He was reaching for the door of the Renault with his free hand. Clara let him get it open, and he saw what she had in her hand. He started to bring his gun up. She shot it out of his hand and it flew in the air while he howled and danced about and nursed his broken hand. His mate prudently scurried out of sight behind the truck.

'I think you can now reverse us out of this stupidity, Tony,' she said. 'I don't want to have to kill either of them.'

No hysterics from her, and he knew she would have shot both of those thugs without too much grieving. The man she had shot was leaning against the side of the truck. His shoulders were hunched, his left hand was holding up his right hand with the lacerated fingers dripping blood. His face was twisted with grief.

'You listen to me,' Clara called out from the car. 'You listen, *hombre* – the next time I see you I will give you a bullet in the belly, and that is my promise. You hear me?'

Tony backed the Renault out of the tangle; they had a crumpled wing, but the car was all right. As they passed the truck Clara leaned out and put two fast shots into its radiator.

'Let them walk,' she said.

'For God's sake,' said Tony fervently, 'put that thing away, it gives me the jitters – you weren't fooling when you said you were a good shot.'

She dropped the gun back into the basket, so casually that it might have been a bundle of knitting.

'They were not very intelligent,' she said. 'There were two of them and one should have been covering the other, then I might have had some difficulty.'

Tony was punishing the Renault, and he was hoping that Clara wouldn't notice how he was sweating – and how lousy his cornering had become all of a sudden.

He did more gear changing than was absolutely necessary, and some of them were pretty rough efforts, but they gave him something to do, and his stomach had stopped churning about so much.

'A little shooting should not upset you,' she said placidly. 'Were you worried for me, Tony?'

'They wanted you, not me,' he said. 'I am never happy when guns are in use. The alarming thing is that they knew where to find us. They must have followed us this morning and we didn't know.'

'So we must be more careful the next time,' she said. 'Were they the men who shot at you last night?'

'I don't know,' he said. 'I honestly don't know, they all look alike to me. Will you be informing the police?'

'Would it to do any good?' Her tone was light. 'They would never catch them. We know the position: Aloysius Morane has sent men here to kill Ambrose, and I am a secondary target.'

'If they had kidnapped you they would have used you as a lever on Halder.'

'There can be no other reason,' she said. 'They could have been watching the villa for some time, that would not be difficult. They knew Ambrose would be taking his walk last night, and this morning they followed us.'

'That suggests a pretty fair organisation,' said Tony. 'There could be quite an army of them.'

'I doubt that,' she said. 'Morane wouldn't risk too many men on a thing like this, he couldn't trust them all to keep their mouths shut. Ambrose is known to be a rich man. The bigger the gang the more chance of a leakage – somebody might try to offer Ambrose a money deal, information for cash. I think this is the work of a small group.'

'They'll try again,' said Tony.

'They will.'

'And they might be lucky,' he said. 'Last night was a bit close. Tell me, does this Morane character see Halder as a threat to his régime? I understand Halder has no organised party left on the island.'

'He has supporters,' she said, 'but he would never provoke a civil war.'

'All he wants is to put a bullet through Morane,' said Tony.

'And that is no secret in Sansovino,' she said. 'Morane knows it, and when the time comes it will happen. Until recently Morane did not know where Ambrose was living, now he knows, and we are seeing the results.'

'Not a healthy outlook,' said Tony. 'I wonder if it's worth it?'

'You must argue that with Ambrose,' she said. 'I have tried, and we are still in Mexico. And now Morane has found us.'

'Ambrose told me about Doctor Luis Almeida,' said Tony. 'He doesn't seem to have been a very good choice as an undercover agent in Sansovino.'

She was silent for a moment. 'The Doctor and I were never in sympathy. He was from the old days in Sansovino, and he thought I was exerting too much influence on Ambrose.'

Tony thought he had the picture: Ambrose's old friend would naturally suspect and resent a woman like Clara.

'You thought he was wrong to go to Sansovino?' he said.

'I respected his courage,' she said. 'We needed information, reliable information. I thought it was unlikely that he would remain at liberty long enough to find out anything useful. We should have sent someone younger, someone with more initiative.'

'Are you looking at me?' he said.

She laughed softly, that laugh he had come to like so much. 'No, Tony,' she said. 'This is not your kind of thing. I would never expect you to take it on.'

'And why not?' he asked. 'You might have been describing me. I'm certainly younger than Almeida was, and I always thought I had initiative. I'm no spy, but couldn't I go there as a tourist? I suppose tourists are allowed in there?'

'They are,' she said. 'There is an airport

now, and tourists are encouraged to come and spend their money. Are you being serious about this?'

'I'm thinking about it,' he said.

'But why would you do it?'

'You think about that as well,' he said.

He didn't look at her, he went on driving for a while, then he stopped and got out on the pretext that he ought to examine the damage to the Renault. It was nothing of any importance.

When he got in again he said, 'Halder said it was a police state, what did he mean by that?'

'Morane and his immediate favourites run everything, including the law court, there is only one; Morane appoints all the officials, and they do as he tells them. He sees himself as a miniature Fidel Castro. Except that Castro does seem to show some care for the ordinary people of Cuba, as long as they follow the party line, while Morane is out for himself alone. The islanders are officially forbidden to leave, although some of the younger ones have smuggled themselves out from time to time, but their families are punished.'

'That sounds like Russia,' said Tony.

'Communism, Socialism, Dictatorship – I

don't know which name best fits Sansovino now,' she said. 'People are directed to the work they have to do, there is no appeal, and the police see that regulations are obeyed. For visitors it is all very different, they have the only luxury hotel on the island reserved for them, with a casino and a night-club of sorts, and the island scenery is very beautiful, so I am told.'

'I imagine Doctor Almeida went in by the back door somewhere?'

'A boat took him in one night,' she said. 'He knew every inlet and bay on the island, and he had some addresses that were thought to be safe, but he couldn't move about openly without being recognised, and he was not the man to remain inconspicuous.'

'Perhaps he was tired of life,' said Tony. 'I'm not.'

She shook her head. 'It was very sad and it achieved nothing. Will you talk to Ambrose?'

'I'll listen to him, but I'm making no promises until I know a lot more. If I don't like the general picture I will opt out and no hard feelings.'

'You are being more than generous,' she said slowly.

'You know why,' he said. 'I have no itinerary that I have to keep to; if tourists are welcomed in Sansovino I don't see why I shouldn't pose as one of them – if I am satisfied that I can do it without risking my neck. One thing I can promise you – I won't go in for any cloak and dagger stuff, I don't have the temperament. I will undertake to keep both eyes and both ears wide open, and I am not quite stupid.'

'You are far from stupid,' she said softly.

He patted her knee. 'You keep on thinking that. It encourages me. I am by nature cautious and unheroic.'

'You do yourself less than justice,' she said.

'A lot of very unusual things have happened since we started this morning,' he said. 'It must be love–'

'Tony, Tony,' she said, and when he glanced at her he liked the expression on her face – the soft curving of her lips and the liveliness in her eyes. Did she look like that at Ambrose Halder? That was a question not to be asked, because he knew the answer.

'Would you agree to do it on those terms?' said Halder.

It was later that evening, after dinner. The three of them were taking coffee in a room

132

that was obviously Clara's sitting-room. There were flowers tastefully arranged, cream rugs on a light polished parquet floor, pastel-shaded drapes and elegant furniture; it was all very charming and quite unlike most of the rooms Tony had seen in the villa. There was no note of austerity here, not like the monastic severity of the room where they had dined, and where the preliminary discussion had taken place.

'When would you want me to go?' said Tony.

'I could have all suitable arrangements made by the day after tomorrow,' said Halder. 'You would be landing in Sansovino late in the afternoon, the regular Caribbean flight from Mexico City; it is normally well booked, but there will be a seat for you. I suggest you travel tomorrow afternoon on a domestic flight to Mexico City, which will allow you time to collect some clothes.'

He smiled briefly and went on, 'It will be essential for you to appear as a visitor with money to spend.'

'And not as a wandering tramp,' said Tony, 'which is what I look like now. It's your money I'll be spending.'

'Hotel accommodation will be reserved for you in Sansovino by the travel office in

Mexico City. You will have nothing to do but sit in the aircraft.'

'Very simple,' said Tony. 'Convince me some more.'

'I will give you some names and addresses which you should learn before you leave here – people it will be safe for you to contact.'

'I'm wondering about that,' said Tony. 'I'm thinking about Doctor Luis Almeida – he also had some safe addresses.'

'It will be different,' said Halder. 'You are going there quite openly, you will be free to move about, as any rich visitor is. Luis didn't have that freedom.'

'And what about the way I leave here?' said Tony. 'The villa is under surveillance, and I was seen with Clara this afternoon, so I am known about. It would make nonsense of it all if one of them follows me.'

'We will not try to hide your departure,' said Halder. 'There would be no point in that. Ernesto will drive you to the airport, and if you are followed you will be seen to leave on the aircraft, so you will no longer be of any interest to them. Does that seem logical to you?'

'It fits,' said Tony. 'When I get to Mexico City I could shave off my beard, in case they've sent a description of me to Sansovino. My passport shows me clean-shaven as a matter of fact.'

'That would be a help,' said Halder, 'and different clothes. There is a police check on landing at Sansovino, but you will meet with no trouble, you will be the kind of visitor they welcome. A spender.'

'American dollars?' said Tony.

'More than you will need,' said Halder.

'That will make a pleasant change.'

Halder gave him a long, thoughtful look. 'Have you convinced yourself you can do it?'

'I am giving it consideration,' said Tony. 'How did it go with the police today? Was it difficult?'

Halder made a rotating movement with one hand. 'Polite probation. They will be happy to see the back of me. It went as I expected.'

'It might have been different if they had known what happened this afternoon down by the beach,' said Tony. 'There is a bandit with a hand he won't be using for while.'

'I could have killed the two of them,' said Clara blandly; an alarming comment from such an elegant lady in her pretty sitting-room. 'But I knew that would arouse too much attention, dead bodies can be an inconvenience.'

'An interesting point of view,' said Tony.

'You were there,' she said, smiling at him. 'it was not a pleasant situation.'

'I disliked it intensely,' he said, matching her smile. 'I am not in favour of shooting. I have a strong pacifist streak in me. Wouldn't it be simpler if you asked for police protection, or am I being naïve?'

'There are two police officers with my men,' said Halder. 'They are in uniform and they have orders to make themselves as conspicuous as possible. They have a police car and they will be in contact with their headquarters all through the night. This is a temporary measure and I am not to expect it to continue, but it will deter Morane's party from any activity around here.'

'I like the sound of that,' said Tony.

'There will be a police escort available when I drive into Acapulco, as I must do tomorrow morning on business. There are financial details that I must attend to, if you decide to make the journey.'

'I'll sleep on it,' said Tony. 'If I go I don't guarantee to find out anything of any great importance, but I'll look and listen, and if I get a reasonable opportunity I might talk to some of the people you say are safe. You may be investing your money to no real purpose except to give me a free trip to Sansovino.'

Ambrose Halder stood up. 'You are an intelligent young man, you have your wits about you, you will be able to assess the way things really are in Sansovino – that is all I want to know, anything you hear that relates to Morane–'

'How long would you expect me to stay?' said Tony.

'I leave that to your discretion,' said Halder. 'Now I will bid you good-night.'

When he had left them alone, Tony said, 'I'm no knight in shining armour, you know why I'm doing this.'

He went over and stood in front of her. After a brief hesitation she stood as well and let him take her into his arms. Before he kissed her she said, 'What happened to Luis Almeida must not happen to you. I could not bear that, Tony.'

'I wouldn't be too keen on it myself either,' he said. 'You'll be glad to see me return?'

She smiled, a warm and radiant smile, and took his face in her hands tenderly.

'I'll come back,' he said. It was a kiss to wipe out the memory of all others. It was like being young again, and in love for the first time. Except they were both much better at it than young love could ever be.

And that night Ambrose Halder did not visit her room when the household slept. They had talked earlier and at some length in his study before dinner, and he knew Clara was not quite the amenable woman she had been before she had met Duchenne.

She fancied herself in love with Duchenne, and Halder knew she would not welcome him in her bedroom. That did not grieve him, not at his age, and Tony Duchenne was going to do what was expected of him.

Halder sat alone in his study, going over the essential details that would ensure a safe passage for Tony Duchenne to where he would be of some use to Ambrose Halder. It had been a lucky accident that had brought them together on that piece of pavement.

Earlier that evening as dusk had been falling the two young men in their dark clothes had watched the unwelcome appearance of the police car with its rotating light. From the shelter of the scrub by the rocks that fringed the road to the villa they had seen the vehicle stop and the men in uniform with rifles get out.

A shoot-out with the pigs in uniform had been no part of their commitment. There had been an uneasy conference between the two. They waited over an hour and the police car was still up there; flashing their torches about in the dark; the pigs were on patrol.

After a while the two of them collected their own guns and crept silently away to the place amid the rocks where they had hidden their car. There was no point in spending another sleepless night watching the *Villa Hermosa*. It was under police protection.

They drove around the outskirts of the town, heading north. In the foothills where the desert spread out they bumped along a dirt track until they came to a dark cluster of old farm buildings, a long way from anywhere. A few tired trees stood around, as shabby as the buildings. They ran the car into a shed behind the main buildings. A dim light came on at the back door. There was no electricity and they were using oil lamps; water came from a pump in the yard. They were all in the country illegally, having come in over the border from Guatemala. Seven men from Sansovino, with orders to kill. Picked men.

Shunkell was at the door, holding the lamp, and a rifle. He was the leader, known as the Captain because of his connection with Morane's less publicised secret police.

He reckoned himself the only real professional in the party, and he had been the first to volunteer for the mission when Aloysius Morane had let it be known that the man who removed Ambrose Halder would have a bright future in Sansovino.

He was young, younger than most of his companions, with a narrow dark face that habitually wore a scowl as though he suspected the rest of mankind had allied itself against him. It put the fear of God into those he had under interrogation.

'What the hell you fellas doing back here?' he demanded. 'You got tired or somethin'?'

'They brought the pigs in, that's what. We figured we was wastin' our time settin' up there all night. We don't aim to mess with no pigs.' The speaker made it seem like a reasonable statement.

His mate backed him up. 'We see a carload of the bastards. We gonna do no good around there, so we come back.'

Shunkell led them into the room they were all using. The two narrow windows had been tightly boarded up, and the air was rank with the smell of men who had been living rough, eating mostly tinned food and sleeping on the stone floor.

On a makeshift bed in one corner, propped

against the wall, nursing his wounded hand, was their first casualty, Bartie. He was the muscle man of the group; he could out-kick and out-gouge and out-savage any normal human. So it was believed. And it was thus doubly galling for him to have had his gun shot out of his hand by a woman, along with the tips of three fingers.

His wound had received only rudimentary treatment from an elderly village doctor who had demanded his money first, since even his aged eyes could see this was no ordinary accident.

Bartie needed liquor to ease his suffering, and Shunkell had put an embargo on hard liquor until they had completed their mission. He had also jumped on any suggestion that the men not on duty might take a car and go into Acapulco for a bit of life. No chicks, no booze. Their combined score to date had been an ignominious zero, and the losing sequence had increased Shunkell's customary sourness with those under his command.

So some harsh words were being used, principally by Shunkell, who did not relish having to report back to Sansovino that they were getting nowhere, and that Halder was now under police protection.

Morale was crumbling, and there were some who thought they should toss it in and go home, and Shunkell had to remind them of the kind of reception they could expect, and also of the unpleasant fact that they would be collecting nothing of the handsome bonus Morane had promised them.

'You fellas want to finish up in the tombs, that's okay with me,' he said, 'but I don't figure I'll join you. I'll stick around; that old bastard Halder, he can't hide behind the pigs all the time – I'll get a shot at him.'

'You were the fella with a gun when we tailed him all over the town,' Bartie reminded him. 'You missed him in clear daylight. I don't reckon you'll get another shot as easy as that.'

'I got unlucky,' said Shunkell shortly.

'Sure did,' said Jakaman. He was their best driver, and mechanic. He had been driving when Shunkell had failed to mow down Halder. He was about Shunkell's age and liked to think that he was the only one Shunkell really trusted. 'That other guy fouled it up jest as I was coming alongside – at first I thought the Captain had blasted the two of them, the way they was lying there on the sidewalk – so I took off real fast.'

'There'll be another chance,' said Shunkell, 'and I'll tell you all this – I wouldn't let any red-headed chick make a fool out of me, you hearing me, Bartie?'

Bartie glared at him, and said nothing. He would be non-effective for the rest of the way; he couldn't hold a gun and he couldn't drive. His hand was giving him hell and he didn't have a drink.

'We're not quitting, so let me hear no more of that talk,' said Shunkell in his most abrasive tone. 'Understood? Tomorrow morning you come with me, Jakaman. We'll give ourselves a nice long careful look at the place, and we won't flip our lids at the sight of a few pigs in uniform, right?'

'You bet,' said Jakaman. 'You figure you might get a shot at him?'

'Unless he stays invisible all the time,' said Shunkell. 'And there's another thing – we ought to know something about this new boy he's got with him. He's no local, that's for sure, and he don't carry a gun, not as far as we know. He's acting like the chick's boy friend, and he lets her do the shooting – that right, Bartie?'

There were some smiles, but Bartie didn't join in. His sense of humour didn't stretch that far.

Shunkell was satisfied that he had reasserted his authority. If they fell down on this job, whatever the excuse, he knew his neck would be on the chopping block first of all. He had volunteered to lead the mission, and Aloysius Morane had no time for failures. Deliver or else...

7

Shunkell was watching the pink-washed villa in the morning sun; Jakaman lay with him in the shade of the rocks. Their view was limited by the ravine and the steeply broken ground between them and the villa, and even with the help of his binoculars Shunkell knew that he wasn't going to get a reasonable shot across that dead ground if Ambrose Halder should be so obliging as to stroll out into the small area of the grounds in their line of sight.

They had ascertained that the police car was no longer up there, and no pigs. One of Halder's men was visible, sitting with a rifle across his legs, smoking and clearly not taking his duty too seriously. Just for practice Shunkell had lined up his rifle with the telescopic sight on the lounging figure; the range was about two hundred yards and there was no kind of movement in the air. If Halder had been the one sitting there he would have been dead.

Shunkell put the rifle aside, and Ernesto,

145

drowsy after two long nights of duty, went on living, and he was plainly bored because nothing had happened to give him any excuse to use his gun and show the *policia* that he wasn't any gardener's boy.

In the course of the next hour Shunkell and Jakaman saw nothing of any interest, except that another man arrived and the sentry got up and both men went out of sight. Then there was the sound of an engine, and they had a quick glimpse of a large black car winding its way up to the villa.

'A Mercedes,' said Jakaman. 'Halder don't have a Merc. Only one fella in it, the driver in uniform, and he was no pig.'

The car was out of sight now, but they could still hear its engine.

'Picking up somebody,' said Shunkell. 'We better get down where we can see who it is.'

They scrambled down the ravine in a hurry to where they had hidden their car, near where the track up to the villa left the road. And they had to wait almost half an hour before the gleaming Mercedes appeared and swung out into the road and put on speed instantly. It was heading for the town. Halder sat in the back, sitting well down in that deep seat so that little of him was visible. Ernesto was with the driver.

They couldn't see if he was armed, because the Mercedes had passed them too quickly.

'Hurry now, boy,' said Shunkell.

Jakaman steered their car out from under the bushes, and by the time they had joined the road the Mercedes was out of sight. Shunkwell had reached back and had his rifle across his lap. He would do this alone, and Jakaman was there to testify how it had been done. It was a good feeling after those flops.

Each time they took a corner, and Jakaman was taking them dangerously close, they looked for that heavy black car, and Shunkell became vitriolic when the road showed them nothing but other vehicles that got in their way and had to be passed.

It was not until they were nearing the town and the traffic had thickened that they saw the Mercedes, and now couldn't hope to get near enough for a shot.

'That fella up there, he's one hell of a good driver,' said Jakaman. 'Got a pretty nice car—'

'Don't make excuses, boy,' Shunkell snapped. 'Get after them!'

'Doin' my best,' said Jakaman.

'So do better!' Shunkell was not happy at seeing this chance slip away.

There were the mid-morning traffic snarl-ups, too many visitors tooling around in luxury American models with time to spend, and crazy cab drivers.

Captain Shunkell could cus as much as he liked, but there was nothing Jakaman could do. If they were picked up for a traffic violation they would be in bad trouble because they didn't have the right papers.

They followed the Mercedes into the business area, and they were still well behind when they saw it stop at one of the tall modern buildings, all concrete and glass. Halder got out and hurried across the wide pavement, and Ernesto came after him. A uniformed doorman held the door open for Halder and gave him a respectful salute.

The driver of the Mercedes remained in the car, in spite of the no-parking zones and other regulations. They would not concern him. There was about him an air of quiet alertness, and he was watching the street and the pavement all the time.

Jakaman drove past with circumspection. 'Looks like a bank,' he said. 'Somethin' like that, smart offices. We can't stop here, and you can't go walkin' around with that shooter–'

'You are a fool,' said Shunkell. 'He is in there on business. He may not be long and

I will get him on the way back. Now drive around a little and come back here, and do nothing silly.'

'Not me,' said Jakaman.

They did the circuit twice, and on the first trip Jakaman did nothing remotely worthy of blame. And the Mercedes had not moved. The second time they coincided with some activity at another bank; there was an armoured security truck unloading currency or bullion, and there was a posse of men in peaked caps and riding breeches and uniform khaki shirts, with shiny black holsters. Part of the road was already under repair, and the security truck blocked the rest.

The flow of traffic was all tangled up while the big money job went on, and the guards were taking no notice of any irate drivers bleeping their hooters. Captain Shunkell had to contain himself, with that rifle hidden under his feet.

When they found that the Mercedes had gone, Jakaman said, a little unwisely, 'So that gives us another big zero. We don't get much goin' for us.'

'Listen,' said Shunkell in his most unpleasant fashion, 'if you had been just a bit sharper, boy, I might have blasted that old bastard's head off before he got here.'

'I don't fix the traffic,' said Jakaman.

'Try the road back to the villa,' said Shunkell. 'We just might pick them up.'

'I could eat somethin',' said Jakaman.

'Young fella like you,' said Shunkell, 'you can do without your chow for a coupla hours, same like me, right? You givin' me an argument?'

On the road back they met the Mercedes, and the driver was alone. Maybe he recognised them, because he put up two fingers as he surged past, on the way back into the town. And he pumped his hooter derisively.

They pulled in to a roadside café for some poor hamburgers and coffee, and not much in the way of happy talk. With the loss of the truck the day before they were down to one vehicle, and on the way out that morning they had brought in Johnny Archer who knew a bit about cars; he had ready cash, and he was to pick up another used job from the dealer who had already done business with them and wouldn't be asking any funny questions about papers and suchlike.

Johnny was okay. Very nearly white. A fat smiling fella. He was to collect some groceries, including cans of beer, as a special concession from Captain Shunkell. Bartie was to be left behind because there was nothing he could do, and later in the afternoon Johnny was to drive the other three out to where the track to the villa started. And Shunkell would tell them what they were to do.

They all knew what would be on Shunkell's mind. The next day he was due to set up their first communication with Sansovino, and he wasn't likely to have anything good to report. A small coaster would fetch up in the bay; she would have a radio link with the island, and Shunkell would go aboard in the afternoon and the coaster would make far enough out to sea and do her transmitting. It was a clumsy arrangement, but the best they could do.

When Johnny arrived he had a large grey Ford. It had blistered paintwork and peeling chrome, but he said it went better than it looked, and it had room for six. He had brought a pack of canned beer and some sandwiches. So the general atmosphere became temporarily a little brighter, and Shunkell was about to dispose his forces so as to make sure that they didn't miss anything they might see up there, when Jakaman came slithering in with the news that the red Renault with the busted wing was coming down, with a passenger who was not Ambrose Halder.

Shunkell detailed Johnny Archer and one of the others to follow in the Ford; if Halder had been the passenger Shunkell would have elected himself as the shadow.

They had covered less than a mile when Tony Duchenne said to Ernesto, 'You can take it nice and easy, that old grey job behind us joined us just now; I think we have picked up some company.'

Ernesto varied his speed, and so did the grey Ford.

'Like me to lose them?' said Ernesto.

'The point is to keep them with us, all the way to the airport.'

Ernesto shook his head, regretting the absence of the competitive element.

'I got it. That's a different pair of fellas from this mornin'–'

'And a different car,' said Tony. 'I think we may be straining their resources, that's a beat-up job following us, so don't make it too difficult for them, and don't forget to give me a nice big public farewell at the airport in case one of them follows me in.'

Johnny Archer was the one. At the airport he hovered around and pretended to study every notice on display, edging all the while as close to Tony and Ernesto as he could get without actually walking on their feet. He looked harmless, a fat slob of a man.

When the flight to Mexico City was called, Tony and Ernesto shook hands.

'Have a nice trip, sah,' said Ernesto. 'Been good to know you.'

'It's mutual,' said Tony. 'Thanks for the lift.'

'You're welcome,' said Ernesto. He waited while Tony joined the queue, and Johnny Archer drifted off a little and then watched until the passengers had all gone.

When Ernesto caught Johnny Archer's wandering eye, Johnny decided it was time to move off. Ernesto caught up with him before they reached the car park. He tugged Johnny Archer round to face him and he poked a hard finger deep into Johnny's belly.

'Listen, fat boy,' he said, 'you worry me, so why don't you take off before I get real sore?'

Johnny Archer backed off and switched on his placatory grin. 'You got the wrong fella, I never seen you before... I don't want no trouble—'

'You got trouble,' said Ernesto, and punched him low in the belly.

Johnny Archer's mate, sitting in the grey

Ford, had watched the brief encounter, and judged it prudent not to interfere. He didn't have a gun, and Ernesto looked like a very tough handful.

Ernesto drove the Renault to the garage which had supplied it and left it there for the wing to be replaced. He collected another car, and on the way back to the villa he was sure he was not being followed. When he made his report to the Senor there was no mention of anybody getting a punch in the belly, because Ernesto considered that had been a personal matter for his own private satisfaction and thus outside the Senor's instructions, so the Senor did not need to know about it.

The flight to Mexico City was a popular one, but for all the interest he was taking in his fellow passengers, Tony Duchenne might have been alone in the aircraft.

That morning at the villa had not been the best of times. He had found Clara distraught and not like the woman who had been in his arms the night before. It had been impossible to get her to himself, even when Halder had gone in to Acapulco about the money. They had had breakfast together, but that had been quite the wrong time to say to her

154

the things he wanted to say.

They had known the night before that he was going to make the trip, and now he felt anything but adventurous. He told himself that it wasn't that he was nervous; there didn't need to be any risk unless he did something particularly stupid, and Halder had given him an exhaustive briefing.

He should look on it as a luxury trip paid for by somebody else, and the political aspects didn't have to weigh with him in the slightest. Ambrose Halder had been friendly and hospitable, and he imagined he owed his life to Tony Duchenne's lightning-quick reaction.

It had been a bogus connection from the start. But with Clara that had been something else again. He couldn't be mistaken about her, otherwise there wouldn't be much point in what lay ahead of him.

So suppose she had been Halder's mistress, that was finished and done with – and the Duchenne record wasn't all that immaculate either; technically he was still a married man.

Of course he could change his mind. He could send the money back to Halder, and ask Clara to come with him and share whatever kind of life they could make for themselves. He could pass the night in Mexico City getting stoned out of his mind...

Watching the trailing edge of the wing out there, he saw the ochre-coloured countryside sliding past. Then they were in cloud, and he found himself memorising those names and addresses Ambrose Halder had given him.

A bizarre situation for a bogus hero. When the stewardess came round he ordered a scotch. There was no 'Johnny Walker', but 'White Horse' was all right. He began to feel a little more relaxed, remembering that very private heap of rocks that she had said they called the *Devil's Tooth*, and the complete happiness of being with her, swimming together, and her legs tight around him before she slipped away. Beautiful. Right out of this world. He closed his eyes and he could still see her and feel her. She had the whole of his mind, irrevocably.

How long did you need before you knew that a woman was the only one for you?

Halder had booked him in a very plushy hotel just outside Mexico City, and he had to do some quick shopping before he felt able to present himself in such opulent surroundings: summer-weight suits, shirts and all the right gear for a traveller who didn't have to watch his expenses. The beard had to go, and he treated himself to the first decent hair-cut he'd had for some months.

The total effect was remarkable, he thought, surveying himself in the changing-room at the shop where he had spent a fair slice of cash. He looked younger and more competent – masquerading as a wealthy young man on his vacation without a care in the world. Money made the difference. Money opened the doors. Everything was smooth and easy when you could pay.

He got through the evening without any discomfort. A late dinner in pleasant sur-roundings, an attentive waiter who had sized him up as a young man on his own and with money to throw around in a strange city. There was a discreet suggestion – perhaps the Senor would care for some amusement, the waiter would be most happy to make arrangements and he was confident that the Senor would not be disappointed ... only high-class ladies, it was understood – if the Senor had a preference?

Tony said no thanks, he would not be interested. The Senor had other plans. A night with a call-girl was not his idea of heaven.

He thought about putting in a call to the *Villa Hermosa*, but he couldn't be sure that he would be able to talk to Clara, and the kind of things he wanted to say to her wouldn't be right with probably Halder listening on some extension. And it would be too childish just to ring and tell them he had arrived. Mexico City was only the beginning of the business.

There were shops in the spacious reception hall, with the usual outrageous prices to be expected in the precinct of a luxury hotel; it was nearly midnight, but there were plenty of people moving about. In the distance somewhere he heard music, with a pronounced Latin-American beat.

He strolled in the hotel gardens for a while; it was cool and fragrant, an oasis of peace and quiet. Good for the spirit.

Wandering farther along he came to the illuminated swimming pool; there were some young people sporting around with a lot of laughter, and one of the girls, a little older than the rest, had a vague resemblance to Clara just because of her auburn hair – she apparently couldn't swim very well and she walked badly. And she really didn't look a bit like Clara. It was pathetic.

He bought himself a drink in one of the

bars, listened in to a variety of conversations without hearing anything of even passing interest, and steadfastly ignored the invitation being flashed to him by a quite decorative lady who was sitting all by herself with a drink she wasn't touching. He wondered if she was one of the waiter's stable.

He went up to his suite; it had all the gadgets imaginable; you could settle in there for the rest of your life, if you didn't mind paying the exorbitant charges. The bathroom even had a vibro-massage thing attached to the wall, for reducing overgenerous hips and bellies. He didn't try it.

He called Room Service and had a pot of coffee sent up, then he sat in an oversize bed and read bits of a book he had been intending to read long ago: Norman Mailer's *Advertisements For Myself.* Some of it suited his mood, and he could put it down without losing any of the flavour.

There was an early start the next morning for the long haul across to Caracas, where the passengers for the Sansovino would transfer to a smaller aircraft because the airport there was not yet ready to receive large jets. Over the Bay of Campeche there was nothing to see because they were already too high and flying in the clouds.

There were empty seats in the aircraft, and Tony had intended to pass the time reading and dozing. But the gentleman sitting across the aisle from him had other ideas. He was one of the talkative ones, a compulsive mixer who felt that Tony must need his company since he was sitting alone.

So he slipped into the vacant seat next to Tony and introduced himself. He was Clement Margolies, the executive vice-president of a firm of realtors with branches all over – Florida, California, New Orleans, etcetera. He was about forty, well dressed, a little overweight, with a round smiling face and shrewd eyes; a seasoned traveller, by his own admission; very friendly.

When he heard that Tony was going on to Sansovino, he said, 'You'll like it there. I'm heading that way myself. Your first visit?'

Tony said it was.

'You're not from the States, Mr Duchenne?'

'Canadian, from Quebec.'

Margolies nodded. 'I thought I recognised the accent. You on business?'

'No,' said Tony. 'Just visiting.'

'A great little island,' said Margolies. 'All set for a boom. You must let me show you around. I know everybody who matters, right up to the top man himself.'

Tony agreed that would be nice.

When the stewardess appeared Margolies had orange juice and made a big business about getting the genuine fruit juice, freshly prepared. Tony settled for a modest coffee since it was a little early for serious drinking, and it was his experience that flying at altitude and hard liquor did him no good except to set his head banging, and he could do without that.

They ran into some turbulence, nothing very violent, but it silenced Margolies for a while, and caused excitement among their fellow passengers in case the wings were about to fall off.

When they had settled back to an even keel, Tony said, 'I take it you've been to Sansovino before?'

'My third trip in less than two months,' said Margolies. 'There's a deal I have cooking down there. Big – and I do mean big.'

'I hope you pull it off,' said Tony politely.

'It looks healthy,' said Margolies. 'I'm getting in early, and, like I said, there's a boom coming in the island. Maybe it won't ever be another Jamaica or Grand Bahamas, but it has possibilities, and the man in the driving seat there has his head screwed on right. Aloysius Morane, he's a smart one all right. I don't suppose you've ever heard of the guy, but he's the only one with any weight on Sansovino.'

Tony listened with interest.

There was only one airfield on the island, and it had only recently been opened, so it was named, predictably, Morane Field.

'He runs everything,' said Margolies.

'That sounds like an old-fashioned dictatorship,' said Tony mildly.

'I wouldn't say that aloud,' said Margolies, 'it's a sensitive subject on the island, and I keep out of politics myself. I deal with Morane on a business basis, and I don't feel I have to bother with anything else. It's his island, and business is business.'

Tony agreed it certainly was.

'He's smart,' said Margolies. 'I'll fix you an interview if you like, you'll find him interesting.'

Tony said he would look forward to it.

Clement Margolies became expansive. 'Y'know, Mr Duchenne, when I was your age I didn't have two dollars to rub together, and now you wouldn't believe what my turnover is.'

Tony assured him it was entirely to his

162

credit that he had made such an outstanding success, a sentiment with which Margolies was in full agreement. He avoided details and Tony didn't press him.

It was later in the afternoon when the executive jet, beautifully appointed and gleaming in the sunshine, made the short flight across the island, with some fifteen well-heeled citizens on board. Most of them were of mature years, with the sophisticated air of those accustomed to travel in comfort. They were a spin-off of the fashionable jet set, with the leisure and the money to break new ground in their quest for the sweet life in the sun.

There had been some talk that one of the younger British Royals was thinking of buying a property on the island, which would really put it on the exclusive map. There was nothing like a Royal Highness to give a resort the social tone that only the selective few would appreciate.

'There she is,' said Margolies.

Sansovino looked very small, in the blue-green sea. They were arriving right on schedule, and as they were on the final approach Margolies pointed out the work still being done on the runways to take the bigger aircraft, and the curve of the bay with the town sprawling up into the hills. Then they were dropping down behind the high ground, to the black tarmac and the concrete, and the shining new administration buildings.

They were a privileged party, and they were accorded a flattering reception from the airport officials. The formalities were minimal, no currency declarations were required, just a perfunctory passport check.

There were two young police officers present, in nice clean uniforms, but they kept in the background. Both of them were armed.

There was a small fleet of cars to transport the visitors to the hotel, less than two miles away. Tony shared with Margolies, who did a short travelogue as they sped along a new road in between the palms.

'About the only decent piece of road in the island,' said Margolies softly. 'Makes a good introduction… Morane is no dummy, first impressions count. You'd need a mule to reach parts of the island, but visitors aren't encouraged to get that far off the track.'

They pulled in at the hotel. It was called the *Tropicana,* which Tony found a little disappointing, he had expected it to be called *Morane House,* or something similar. It was set in spacious grounds with pleasant gardens – there was a large main building, and a series of bungalows or chalets dotted about in the shade of the trees, but not so near each other as to spoil privacy. Beyond the main buildings there were tennis courts, and what looked like a row of loose boxes for horses. There would also be a golf course somewhere in the area.

Since their party was a small one, Tony was offered a choice of accommodation, a suite in the main building, or one of the bungalows usually reserved for couples. He chose the bungalow; it might offer more freedom to move without being noticed by the staff, of whom there seemed to be a surplus, making themselves available wherever one looked.

Margolies caught up with him as he followed his luggage along the path between the beds of flowers.

'We're neighbours,' said Margolies. 'They've put me in the shack next to yours.'

'Cosy,' said Tony.

'Right now I have a business date with the top man,' said Margolies. 'When I'm through with him we might take a look around.'

'Why not?' said Tony. The more local information he could pick up the better, and

Clement Margolies was very ready to impart information.

'If you fancy a swim before the sun goes, there's a cliff lift at the end of the gardens, it'll take you down to the private beach.'

'Every home comfort,' said Tony.

'Be seeing you,' said Margolies. 'Wish me luck, that Morane is a hard one to nail down.'

'Nail him down,' said Tony. 'Good and proper.'

8

Aloysius Vincent Morane was a tall un-smiling man. Like most of the islanders, he was a mixture of many races, with the Spanish strain predominating. There was a little of the negro in his appearance; his skin was a pale chocolate brown, he had a thin nose, smooth black hair that had never been kinky, a tight mouth that seldom relaxed, and dark eyes that gave nothing away of what might be going through his mind.

Few people had ever seen him laugh, and nobody had ever seen him weep. He was self-contained, and sure of his destiny.

His mother had been a worker in the cane fields, when there was work to be done, which was not always. As a boy Aloysius regularly knew what it was to go to bed on an empty stomach; his mother was of a generous nature, with the result that Aloysius was never quite sure who was his father.

Unlike the other boys in his village, he was inquisitive and given to asking the kind of questions to which his elders had no convincing answers, such as why some folks were rich and others were not. He had soon exhausted the resources of the village school and its master, and the parish priest was already foretelling a bad future for him unless he changed his ways and learned to respect those whom the Almighty had placed over him, such as the excellent Senor Ambrose Halder and his family.

There were some minor brushes with authority, for heinous crimes like daubing slogans on walls where God-fearing citizens would be sure to see them, and scattering inflammatory pamphlets that had been printed outside the island, inciting the workers to rise and claim their rights by overthrowing their tyrannical landlords.

Young Morane had become a nuisance, a fiery, skinny youth who liked nothing better than to provoke a noisy argument in a public place, even in the churchyard after Sunday Mass. And he had nothing to do with the local girls, which placed him apart from his contemporaries.

When his mother died, he did what had always been in his mind, he left Sansovino for Cuba, and there he really did learn his business. He discovered in himself a talent for manipulating people, and for keeping a sharp eye on all the details that make for success. He could talk and coax and drive, and he believed in what he was doing. Fidel Castro might have been aware of him as just another zealous volunteer, but Morane was learning all the time the techniques he was going to need. He grew up. He knew he was going to make his mark.

He paid several visits to Sansovino, at first in secret, and later openly, with Ferdinand Brea, his lieutenant and another exile from the island. Brea was no self-educated peasant; he had attended the High School in Caracas, and then the University. His father had been a farmer who had drifted into insolvency, and young Brea had arrived in Cuba soon after Morane.

They made a good team, and when they decided to move back to Sansovino, with some money to spend and a clear idea of what they were about, they soon began to make themselves felt. They were no longer amateurs, content to make futile gestures against the government. They knew the power of an organised minority, and the effect of the right propaganda. Sansovino was ripe for the plucking. It took them just a little over a year. An exercise in political take-over technique.

It had been done quickly and with the minimum of bloodshed, a tribute to the thoroughness and the efficiency of the campaign that had led up to it, and perhaps also to the apathy of most of Sansovino's people. The one unfinished piece of business had been the person of Ambrose Halder, who should have been the first to die.

However, the arrival of that decrepit old fool, Doctor Luis Almeida, had provided a solution. Almeida had been taken the day after he sneaked into the island, and Morane and Brea had given him personal attention, off and on for a day and two nights. They had employed some of the refinements they had seen in practice in Cuba, and the old man had been nothing but a gibbering idiot by the time they had done with him.

But he had told them what they wanted to know, and he had been buried in an unmarked grave in the prison compound. And the execution squad had set out, under the command of the one who was thought best fitted for the job, Shunkell.

Now, in his office, Aloysius Morane was reading the report Ferdinand Brea had just brought him, the first report from Shunkell, and it had not made good reading. Nothing had been accomplished.

'If I were you,' said Brea,' I would call them back.'

'You are not me,' said Morane.

His wide desk was bare, except for a signed portrait of Fidel Castro.

'He has police protection,' said Brea.

'There are seven of them,' said Morane. 'They have guns and they have money. I do not see the difficulty. He is the last of that family, one man who should now be dead. Do they need an army to do it! Have a message sent to Shunkell; I do not want to see him until it has been done.'

'The aircraft has come in from Caracas,' said Brea. 'The American is waiting to see you.'

'He thinks we are fools here,' said Morane. 'I do not need to see him again. His money is from the Mafia. If we let him in here we lose control. I know well what he is after – we allow them a small concession, and then what happens? they bring in more and more of their people, they take over more and more of our business, and they will do with us what they have done elsewhere where they think there are easy profits. They bring in a bad element. They think they can buy everybody. But they cannot buy you and they cannot buy me. They promise this and they promise that, and they will be stealing our money with their percentages and their concessions, they will drain it away before we even see it – that is their way of doing business. We need financing, but not at their price.'

Morane's voice had remained flat and un-emotional. After the first visit from Margolies, they had done some thorough checking; Brea had been back to Havana to find out what was known about this American with his grand and persuasive plans for developing Sansovino into another playground in the sun. And they had been reliably informed that Margolies was no ordinary real estate man; he had figured in deals that had converted some of the Bahamas into little more than gangster resorts; the capital he had talked about so fluently came from very doubtful sources – Mafia money from the rackets.

'He is an operator, as they call them,' said Morane. 'He has a glib tongue, and he thinks he is dealing here with simple-witted peasants.'

He stood up and walked across to the wide window from which he had his favourite view – of the palatial hotel, and the bay; the slums clinging to the lower slopes down into the town were hidden by the landscaped grounds that surrounded Morane's headquarters; high walls and guards ensured his privacy, and all visitors were rigorously searched before they were allowed into the Presence.

'We are not going to let ourselves be cheated out of all this,' said Morane. 'We have been through too much together.'

'We have,' said Brea.

'How many arrived this afternoon?'

'Fifteen, including the American. Spoilt rich people. Two of the women look interesting.'

Morane turned back from the window. 'You will leave them alone,' he said. 'If they wish to fornicate we keep healthy young men on the hotel payroll. You have a position here, and you have a wife.'

'She is fat, and she is always too pregnant,' said Brea, 'but it will be as you wish.'

Morane dismissed the matter of sex; it had never governed his life; he had never married and he had never had any kind of a real liaison with a woman. There was a secretary on the staff, a clever and devoted girl who lived in a bungalow in the grounds with an ailing mother who found it convenient to ignore the infrequent nights when her

173

daughter had been summoned by telephone from the Residence to work late, very late. She was a strapping figure of a girl, with healthy appetites, but the occasional interludes with Morane were brief and without any show of tenderness on his part. A coupling of male and female, largely in silence, a brisk physical contact during which she was expected to remain quiescent. No sentimental talk in bed, no promises of a future. She had a limited use and there could be no future for her, but she was being well paid and she could buy herself a husband when Morane had no more need for her.

Ferdinand Brea, on the other hand, had been an active womaniser from his youth; he had seduced a priest's pious housekeeper when he was no more than sixteen, and the mere sight of a pretty woman was enough to stir him; among the *compadres* in Cuba he had been a great success, and as Morane's right-hand man on the island he had been finding many opportunities – there had been gratifying episodes with some of the lady visitors, with or without their husbands.

'You think too much of what is between your legs,' said Morane. 'Any animal in the fields can do it.'

Brea smiled. This was no new conversation. 'With me it is love. But I never let it interfere with the work I do.'

'The day that happens,' said Morane, 'you and I become strangers.'

'Never,' said Brea. 'What would you like me to do about Margolies?'

'He is not here by my invitation,' said Morane. 'Let him wait our convenience. Whenever I look out there at the *Tropicana* I am thinking of all that we must do.'

'We have made a good start,' said Brea. 'It is a fine hotel.'

'We will build a better one on the other side of the island,' said Morane. 'Then we will arrange to sell plots of land to the right kind of people, the ones who can afford to spend their winters here; luxury villas for very rich people. We will own the company, we will share nothing with any Mafia mob … no percentage, no rake-off.'

'The man from the London banking house arrives tomorrow,' said Brea. 'Margolies will not be happy to find he has competition.'

'I would rather accept financing from London than from the Mafia,' said Morane. 'London bankers deal like gentlemen; there will be no cheating with them, and they are sufficiently interested to send one of their men on a private flight to see us. I take that as a very favourable sign.'

'It shows more than interest,' said Brea. 'London merchant banks are run by conservative people, from all I have ever heard, and to send one of their experts all this way must mean that they feel we have something worth their while.'

'We have a sound proposition,' said Morane. 'All we need is adequate financing.'

'Come to Sansovino in the sun,' said Brea, 'but only if you have a lot of money to spend.'

'The island is quiet and we have it all under our control,' said Morane. 'It is ready for development, and now is the time. When we have shown this Charles Brockway what he needs to see here, then I intend to visit London myself to take the matter further with his principals.' He unlocked a drawer in his desk and took out a folder. They both knew its contents by heart, since they had drawn it up together – the plans for the island's future.

'We will go over it again,' said Morane. 'Get a chair and join me.'

'Shall I send Margolies away first?' said Brea. He did not share his chief's ability to work long hours without food or drink, and this was a session that might last well into the night. Morane kept nothing in his office in the way of refreshment, and Brea was hoping to pick up a quick drink on the pretext of seeing Margolies off the premises.

'We can let him wait a little longer,' said Morane. 'There is one matter concerning him, he is to have no telephone calls out of the island as long as he is here. We are shutting the door in his face, politely of course.'

'He is likely to make a fuss,' said Brea.

'Then we must find an empty cell,' said Morane, 'where he can cool off.'

After having passed an uneventful evening, Tony Duchenne was sitting up in bed reading. There had been an excellent meal in the *Tropicana's* attractive dining-room, where the glass doors had been open to the cool night air and the drifting scent of the flowers; he had looked in on the casino, where he had rapidly dropped three hundred and ten dollars; he had seen some of the local talent, boys as well as girls, all shiny brown and lissom, going through exotic routines in the cabaret; and girls, as near naked as made no difference, performing the near-impossible as limbo dancers, and very nice too.

From his casual observation of the scene,

he concluded that nobody need go to bed alone except by choice.

He had circulated and had done a little discreet drinking, in the course of which he had exchanged social chit-chat with fellow guests, and nobody had so much as mentioned the name of Aloysius Morane – or Ambrose Halder for that matter. They were rich fun people, and Sansovino, delightfully unspoilt, was their playground.

He had avoided being recruited into a poker school that looked as though it would be active throughout the night. He could see little point in travelling so far and at considerable expense just to sit in cigar smoke and lose his money at poker.

Margolies hadn't appeared; he had probably been dining with Aloysius Morane; he was the man on the inside track, it would appear, and thus worth cultivating.

There were footsteps outside, and his bell chimed. Margolies was at the door. He looked harassed and grim.

'I'm having trouble with my phone,' he said. 'Mind if I try yours?'

'Help yourself,' said Tony. 'Did you have a good evening?'

'Lousy.' Margolies lifted the phone, each bungalow had one. He rang the hotel exchange. 'This is Clement Margolies, about that call I've been trying to put in, Miami, Florida, person-to-person … what's that? Listen, that's not good enough … okay, okay.'

He put the phone down. 'That's the third time I've tried in the last hour. They can't put me through, some technical nonsense, they say. You'd think Florida was the other side of the world. Incompetent bastards.'

'You look a little under the weather,' said Tony. He went over to the drinks cabinet that came with the bungalow, comprehensively stocked.

'I'll take rye,' said Margolies.

Tony brought over the bottle and a glass. 'Excuse me if I don't joint you,' he said. 'I took on all I need earlier. What happened to you? I looked for you–'

'I've been given the runaround,' said Margolies. 'I've been sitting on my butt all evening, just waiting like some goddam servant. You'd think they never heard of me.' He swirled his drink around in the glass. 'I wonder what was behind it? I never even got to see Morane. He was busy, that was all the apology I got. Too busy to see me! I don't like that kind of treatment from anybody. I'll be back there tomorrow morning even if I have to kick the door in.'

'Perhaps he changed his mind?' said Tony.

'It was a brush-off,' said Margolies. 'Nobody does that to me.'

'But I thought you were on such excellent terms,' said Tony.

'I thought so as well,' said Margolies. 'I knew he was a tricky bastard, but I never expected him to try to put a fast one on me. It's a squeeze, and my associates won't like it when I tell them, they won't like it one little bit. And now the goddam phones don't work!'

'Very inconvenient,' Tony agreed. 'It was important business you were hoping to discuss with Morane?'

Margolies shot him a shrewd look over the edge of his glass. 'You could call it that.'

'I don't know much about the world of business,' said Tony, 'but I suppose it's like anything else, you have to expect snags somewhere. You'll probably get a call from Morane tomorrow, he'll want to see you–'

'That wasn't the message I got,' said Margolies. 'I can leave Sansovino any time I like, that was what I heard from Ferdinand Brea, he's Morane's number one man. They want me out. When I got steamed up about being kept waiting all evening, Brea said I could pass the night in a police cell if I didn't like the way they operated, and he wasn't fooling.'

Margolies sloshed out another drink, his round face tight with anger at the memory of the insult.

'So what are you going to do?' said Tony.

'I'll stick around,' said Margolies. 'You bet I'll stick around.' He took his liquor fast and slammed the glass down. 'There's too much at stake to let myself be dumped like that, and I want to know what the hell is going on here. Somebody has put a fix in, and I'm going to know who and what ... the outfit I represent doesn't get pushed around by any bunch of *peons* like Aloysius Morane and Ferdinand Brea.'

'A difficult situation for you,' said Tony sympathetically. 'Morane runs this place, and he'll be a dangerous man to upset; in your position I don't think I'd risk it. But then, I'm not the adventurous type.'

'I've handled bigger men than Morane.'

'I'm sure you have,' said Tony. 'But this is different, you're on his territory, it's all loaded against you.'

'I'm not running,' said Margolies. 'I didn't make my pile by taking off when it looked tough; besides, I have my associates to think of ... hell, I sure wish I could get to a phone

181

that works.'

'They'll have them working by the morning,' said Tony.

'I wouldn't put any money on it,' said Margolies. 'There's a bad smell around here.' He stood up. 'Sorry to bust in here so late and bend your ear.'

'No bother,' said Tony, and walked his visitor to the door. 'I wished you luck before, now I really do mean it.'

'You're okay,' said Margolies, with the ghost of a smile on his plump face. 'You listen good. Thanks. See you in church.'

After he had gone along the path, Tony looked at his phone, and thought of trying to put in a call himself, just to see if that technical trouble was genuine or restricted to outside calls, especially those made by Clement Margolies. He couldn't think of anybody to call, except Clara, or Halder, and that would be a stupid risk to take. If Morane had the island under tight control, a night call to Acapulco would be asking for trouble.

He had nothing to report: he had arrived and he had seen nothing of Sansovino but the airport and the hotel; for all he knew, the island could be seething with unrest. Perhaps tomorrow he might begin to assess the position. Behave like a wealthy visitor, wandering hither and yon, where the natives might be friendly to a stranger with a thick wallet and a chatty disposition.

He didn't expect to discover anything that would justify the trip, but it wasn't his money he was throwing around.

He climbed back into bed, and he thought for a while about Doctor Luis Almeida, lost without trace. Not a good omen.

9

When Margolies arrived at Morane's splendid new headquarters, the ornate gates were shut, and there were three men on duty in military uniforms and with guns; one of them seemed to be an officer, a dapper young man with a rakish peaked cap and wearing a shiny Sam Browne and a holster with the flap undone.

Margolies got out of his car and announced himself; he had important business to discuss with His Excellency, so if they would kindly open those gates and let him in...

'I regret, Senor,' said the officer, 'you may not enter. I have my orders from His Excellency himself. There is nobody available to see you, they are at the airport.'

'I can wait until they come back,' said Margolies.

'That is not possible. I must ask you to move your vehicle. It is not permitted to you to wait here.'

The two soldiers had been following the

conversation with open interest; they had automatic rifles, and they had ranged themselves one on each side of their officer.

Clement Margolies had faced a hostile gun before, and more than once in his colourful career, but never against such odds. Those two boys looked too ready to stitch holes in him if their officer gave the word.

So, 'I'll call another time,' said Margolies.

'You will not be allowed in,' said the officer. 'If you should choose to make a nuisance of yourself, Senor, I have clear orders—'

Margolies got back into his car, and the officer gave him a very correct salute as he drove off. When he was out of sight, Margolies stopped the car and considered the position. Before leaving the hotel he had tried again to put a phone call through, and with the same result as the night before, and the operator hadn't even pretended to be apologetic. The freeze was really on.

The airport? Was Morane taking a trip outside the island? That might be worth knowing. He drove to the junction, the right fork led to the *Tropicana*, left to the airport. He drove left.

He reached the airport just in time to see Morane and Brea walking across the tarmac with a stranger in a linen suit; there was a small twin-jet on the runway, trundling slowly towards the hangar. Under an armed guard there was a black Mercedes, the head-of-state model, the one with bullet-proof glass and a reinforced body that you could practically drive through a brick wall; seating six or seven, with a pair of jump-seats for the bodyguards. Margolies had ridden in one many times, in those raw old days when there were contracts out and the torpedo boys were after him.

He watched with much interest as Morane and his party got into the car, and the character in the linen suit was being given the V.I.P. treatment. When the Mercedes left there was an armed guard up in front by the driver, and another car followed with more men.

The activity was over. And nobody paid any attention to Margolies, standing idly in the sun with his jacket slung over his shoulder. Morane Field was far from busy now.

He strolled in through the administration area, and was not challenged. There was no tannoy blaring out information about flight schedules, no queues of travellers, none of the noisy bustle of an airport doing good business. Adequate new buildings, and a sleepy staff.

They would have to change all that pretty smartly, once they got a working interest in the island. Morane Field would have to earn its keep. There was a refreshment lounge, with nobody on duty; he could hear the hired help chatting in the kitchen; he left them to it.

With no trouble at all he found his way out to the tarmac. The twin-jet was now in the hangar, and mechanics were standing around looking at it. Margolies found a bench in the shade of the main buildings and sat, like one who had every right to be there. On any properly run airport he would have been eased out by security men.

Up to his right there was the control tower, with glass all around. That was probably the one place in the whole goddam island where a radio message would be sent without interference – and he knew he would never get the chance to use it, no matter how much cash he offered. He couldn't see anybody on duty, but they would have somebody on watch, even with a sloppy outfit like Morane Field.

He thought about sauntering across to the hangar, to find out about the visitor who had caused such a fuss. Then he saw that one of the mechanics was coming his way. Margolies waited to be evicted. The mechanic was a young man, and he gave Margolies a pleasant smile.

'A nice morning, Senor,' he said. 'You are admiring our field?'

'Very nice,' said Margolies. 'Not a lot of traffic though.'

The young man waved one arm. 'When the runway is extended, it will be busy then. You are a visitor?'

'Arrived yesterday,' said Margolies. 'Quite an island you have here.'

The young man joined him on the bench. Margolies brought out his cigarettes, and the young man was immediately impressed by the case and the lighter Margolies used.

'You will be staying at the *Tropicana*, Senor? That is a most comfortable hotel. One day perhaps I will visit there. I am Juan Cabrera.'

'Clement Margolies, very nice to meet you.'

'*Americano?*'

'That's right,' said Margolies.

'I would much like to go there and work, I am a first-class mechanic, Senor. There would be work for a man like me?'

'Plenty of work,' said Margolies. 'Don't you like it here?'

Juan Cabrera's shrug was eloquent. He was young and he was ambitious, and for him Sansovino was plainly no paradise in the sun. This rich *Americano* might be the one to help him to get out.

Without hurrying and with much finesse, Margolies steered the conversation the way he wanted it to go, and very soon he had the name of the eminent visitor in the twin-jet. It was Charles Brockway, from London, England; a most important man who had come to talk with Aloysius Morane himself. What about? Juan could only repeat the rumours, that there were going to be big developments on the island very soon. Morane would be going to England with the visitor, that much was sure because the arrangements had been made. Probably tomorrow.

The Englishman was not staying at the *Tropicana*. He was Morane's guest, at the official residence.

If the Senor would like to go fishing, Juan had a cousin with an excellent boat, and he would be most happy to fix a day's fishing for the Senor.

Margolies said that sounded like a good idea, one day soon. He would get in touch with Juan when he had a free day.

'I am always here, Senor,' said Juan. Then,

'Would you wish me to reserve the boat for you? There is much demand for it with the visitors at the hotel.'

Margolies smiled and took out his wallet. Juan had made his sales pitch. 'If you happen to hear that Senor Morane is definitely going to England tomorrow, ring me at the hotel – I'll be available between eight and nine tonight.' He folded three ten-dollar bills and slipped them into Juan's breast pocket. 'Can do?'

'Bet your life,' said Juan.

'This is a little business matter, between you and me, okay?' said Margolies. 'There will be no trouble for anybody, and if I don't hear from you I'll meet you in the car park tomorrow morning about this time. Then we can fix that fishing trip.'

As he drove away from the airport Clement Margolies was in the frame of mind that in his more active days would have ensured a concrete burial for the opposition. So Aloysius Morane was shopping elsewhere for his financing. That explained everything. Margolies had generated so much heat inside himself that he had to stop the car and wipe his face and neck, and if Morane had suddenly appeared on the roadside

Margolies would have shown him what it meant to play tricks on the man sent by the syndicate.

It had been years since Margolies had done any of his own killing, he was too far up in the organisation now, but he had an automatic, and none of Morane's uniformed monkeys would be fast enough. After a little while, he had cooled down. A little.

This wasn't going to go down well. Even a top man in the syndicate couldn't afford to fall flat on his face like this. Outsmarted by a goddam peasant who had grabbed himself the front seat. You just couldn't trust these ignorant bastards. Millions of easy dollars for somebody else, and after he had done all the spadework.

He couldn't get a message out. He would try again, but he understood the pattern now – Morane had it all tied up. So there was no point in staying on the island any longer.

Charles Brockway, from London, England, given preferential treatment all right. V.I.P. reception and accommodation in Morane's house. Somebody outside had to know about him, and the people he represented. It was unfortunate that the syndicate's long arm didn't any longer reach into London. The British police had spoilt all that. Deporting the club operators, and so on.

The gambling junkets didn't run any more. But anyone who thought the *Cosa Nostra,* or the syndicates, didn't operate, didn't know what they were talking about. A low profile, that was the modern thing. Which made a deal like the one they had thought up for Sansovino all the more desirable, and profitable.

Tony Duchenne had passed an uneventful morning. He had called at the bungalow next door, and had found Margolies had gone somewhere, quite early. He had watched a little tennis, but it was garden party stuff, and he wasn't invited to join – they were probably being nice and understanding about his leg.

He went for a swim at the private beach; it was pleasant enough, but he was the odd man out among two married couples from the better parts of Boston; one of the women was passable when she stopped acting the lady.

He sun-bathed for a while until it got too fierce, then took the lift back up the cliff. He sat in the shade of a summer-house in the gardens and told himself that he ought to make some kind of a plan of campaign. So far he had discovered nothing about the island that he didn't know before he had landed at Morane Field. There was no local source of news, like a newspaper. He would have to get out and do his own foraging. Act like a real tourist and talk to the people on the island, if he could find any of them ready to talk ... an inn, or a pub, some place like that, in the evening.

He didn't think he was going to be very good at it. Secret agent business. He had told Halder that wasn't his style. Sansovino was peaceful enough on the surface, whatever discontents might be bubbling underneath. He might check on some of the addresses Halder had given him, but he promised himself that he would be ever so discreet. The Duchenne neck would not be exposed. Not bloody likely.

He made an enquiry about transport, and he was told there was a variety of vehicles he could choose from, chauffeur-driven if required, and since he estimated that the island was less than twelve miles long at the most a chauffeur would be superfluous. He collected a map, which the reception clerk told him was the only official and up-to-date guide to Sansovino; included in it were some glossy pictures of the recommended spots to visit. Compliments of the *Tropic-*

ana, Senor.

He was relaxing in his bungalow when he saw Margolies return next door, and he went along to suggest a drink before lunch.

'I've been screwed,' said Margolies bitterly. 'Me, Clement Margolies! Played for a sucker from hell to breakfast by Aloysius Morane! Can you imagine that? Twice I come here and we have nice long friendly discussions; I give him details, plans and figures, all the business, I have the financial backing and we have the know-how to make this little island a real money-spinner ... we've done it before and we can sure as hell do it here.'

Margolies picked up a black briefcase, hefted it, and threw it violently across the room.

'What a goddam waste of time! You know what happened this morning? They rolled out the red carpet at the airport to welcome a guy from England, Charles Brockway, come to talk business with Morane – they give him a big reception, Morane and Brea, and they whip him off to stay in Morane's place. I also hear that Morane will be going to London himself soon – which leaves me where? Tell me that?'

'On the outside looking in,' said Tony. 'Are the phones still out of order?'

'Give you two guesses,' said Margolies, 'and you'll be right both times.'

'You've been diddled, to coin a phrase,' said Tony. 'There's been some sharp practice at your expense – you didn't have a contract with Morane?'

'Exploratory discussions,' said Margolies briefly.

'And this Charles Brockway from London has edged you out?' said Tony. 'I'm sorry. I'd say you've had a raw deal all round.'

'I ought to have some muscle sent in here to straighten the guy out,' said Margolies. 'We don't take that kind of treatment from anybody.'

'And Morane is off to London?' said Tony.

'Maybe tomorrow,' said Margolies. 'I have to get out of this place fast–'

There was the sound of a vehicle stopping nearby, the tramping of feet along the path, and the bell rang.

'I didn't tell you a thing, right?' said Margolies, and went to open the door.

The police officer was the one who had stopped him at the gates of Morane's residence, and behind him were two armed guards.

'You will come with me, Senor,' said the officer.

196

Margolies picked up his jacket. He looked unruffled. 'You mean I'm under arrest?' he said. 'What's the charge, or don't you guys bother with crap like that?'

The officer smiled. 'You are being offensive. It is very stupid of you. My orders are to take you with me, Senor. You will make a nuisance of yourself no longer.'

The two guards moved in and stood beside Margolies. Margolies nodded at Tony and the guards marched him out. The officer glanced at Tony. 'I trust you are enjoying your visit to Sansovino, Senor.'

'I was until a minute ago,' said Tony. 'What has he done?'

'He has been making a nuisance of himself,' said the officer.

'And you arrest people for that?' said Tony. 'Isn't that a bit rough?'

The officer was at the door. He turned. 'I am not required to explain things to you, Senor, but I will tell you that we do not permit our visitors to offer bribes to our engineers at the airport, and we do not permit visitors to ask questions about matters that no longer concern them. That man has been doing both of these things this morning at our airport. He is a friend of yours?'

'I'm in the next cabin,' said Tony. 'We

197

came over on the plane yesterday. I'd never seen him before then.'

The officer gave him a long speculative look. 'This man is an American gangster, did you know that, Senor?'

'Good heavens, no,' said Tony.

'We do not like our visitors to abuse our hospitality,' said the officer. 'You should be more careful in choosing your companions, Senor.'

'I will,' said Tony fervently. The officer took a last look around the room, saw the briefcase where Margolies had thrown it, and picked it up.

'Not mine,' said Tony, and followed the officer out.

They were taking no chances with Clement Margolies. They had him in a truck with a guard on each side, and Tony judged it more prudent to remove himself from the scene, because that young officer was watching him as though not quite sure of him.

Back in his own bungalow he found he had lost his appetite for lunch. Ambrose Halder had particularly wanted to know about Morane's movements, and Tony hadn't expected to get any information – but now he could tell Halder that Morane would be away from

Sansovino, that he would be making a business trip to England, and that was surely something that Halder would want to know.

So what was the point in staying any longer on the island? There was also the unfortunate matter of Clement Margolies – he was probably in jail, and Tony might be under suspicion himself because he had been in Margolies' company. A tricky situation. The solution was to get out as conveniently as he could. And without making it too obvious that he was running away.

He had provisionally booked in at the *Tropicana* for a week. If he left tomorrow afternoon on the return flight to Caracas he could pretend that the heat was proving too much for him. He would have a wealthy visitor's whims and fancies, and he could pay to indulge them.

He would stay within the hotel grounds, and he would complain that his knee was giving him hell. He went up to lunch, and when he was asked what all that business had been about Margolies he said the chap had run into trouble with the police, and that was all he knew.

He passed the afternoon lazing in his bungalow with the air-conditioning full on and the blinds drawn against the glare; he tried to read but found it impossible to concentrate; an uneasy afternoon all through.

Obviously Margolies had been under surveillance, or he had been informed on. That officer had said he was an American gangster, and Tony found that more than likely – all that talk about his associates, and bringing in some muscle to straighten Morane out, that had been gangster talk.

He was dozing when he heard a car stop at the end of the path. He peeped through the curtains, and his stomach lurched when he saw the troopers coming down, two of them, and again with the officer. But they went into Margolies' bungalow, which was a considerable relief. They would be searching it, of course. They were inside there about half an hour, and when they came out each of the troopers carried a case, the officer had nothing. He stood for a while in the sun, looking towards Tony's bungalow, and Tony was very happy to see him join his men and drive off. It wasn't only the heat that brought the sweat to Tony Duchenne.

The *Tropicana* was proving to be no luxury rest-cure in the sun. Not for Tony Duchenne. What had happened to Margolies might easily happen to him, a prospect he found far from comforting. A discreet and speedy departure was the thing. Tomorrow at the latest.

10

As the sole commander of a small force operating a long way from home in unfamiliar territory, Shunkell was having plenty of trouble. There had been that succinct and uncompromising order from Sansovino, demanding immediate results and ignoring his excuses.

In a savage mood he had tried to inject some enthusiasm for the mission in his men, and some notion of military discipline, and his efforts had not gone down too well. Johnny Archer and Bartie had decamped with their second car and most of their stores, and of the four men left the only one still inclined to obey orders was Jakaman. The other three reckoned the job was beyond them and they didn't see any profit in crawling about trying to get a shot at a fella who never showed himself.

Disaffection was spreading, and Shunkell had cursed and threatened them in vain.

So, with Jakaman he had taken himself off for another visit to the scene. They had arrived before dawn, and they had made one more survey. Shunkell was going to find a spot where he could see more of the villa than just a portion of the front wall, even if he had to risk exposing himself. All through the previous day they had watched from comparatively safe places; they had seen some of the staff going about their duties, and the woman in the garden in front. Ambrose Halder had been invisible.

They crawled and slithered and clambered; they had come into the danger area – if there had been any daylight any man on sentry duty there must have seen them.

Shunkell found a narrow fissure in the rocks, and the villa was no more than a hundred yards away. He could see windows and doors, and much of the garden. But he was open to view himself.

Jakaman gathered scrub and whatever he could find, and covered him over, then retreated to a less exposed position lower down the hill.

Shunkell was lying on rock, broken rock with jagged edges, and no amount of careful wriggling eased his position. He had a canteen of water, some bread and cheese, and the rifle. He could lie there all day, immobile, waiting for just one shot.

When the light improved he saw a man lazily making his way up from the lower end of the garden; he had a rifle under his arm; he must have been on duty down there when they arrived, and he hadn't noticed a thing. That made Shunkell feel better. He could have put a bullet between the fella's shoulder blades without even trying.

A few minutes later another man was squatting on the flat roof of the garage, with his back against the low parapet; he wore a wide straw hat, and his rifle lay on the roof beside him. Shunkell could have removed him as well.

The sun came up and the heat increased. Shunkell could feel those rocky edges biting into his ribs; by mid-morning he was soaked in sweat and the insects were giving him some private torment. Any movement he made threatened to dislodge his camouflage, and he was getting little fresh air. This was his last chance, and he would stay with it all day if he had to. He drank some of the tepid water but he couldn't eat anything.

He kept his vision clear and his finger supple, and the rifle was there ready by his cheek; a dozen times over he had practised drawing on the door of the villa, sliding the thin muzzle of the rifle through the branches that covered him in front.

The woman came out and stood in the sunshine, looking around the garden. They said she was Halder's whore. She wore a light dress and a white hat like a sombrero, and she carried a basket. She began to cut some flowers. The door she had come out of was open and Shunkell could just see a shadowy figure inside there. The woman turned towards the door and held up a bunch of flowers and Shunkell could hear her voice, she laughed and said something.

And he saw the sure way to get Halder out into the open. It had to be Halder in there.

He waited for the woman to stop moving, lined her up in his sights, and fired, and she fell down among the flowers.

Halder came out of the door, shielding his eyes against the sun. Shunkell should have waited, just a split second longer. He fired and saw Halder stagger against the door and he knew he had been too soon.

So he thrust the branches out of his way and stood up for a final shot. Below him Jakaman shouted.

Ernesto was the guard on the garage roof. He had been bored, sitting there with nothing to do in the morning sun. Nothing had happened during the night, and nothing was going to happen now.

The first shot had him leaping to his feet. The second had him searching the rocks in front of him, his rifle poised. When Shunkell showed himself, Ernesto began to pump bullets at him, very rapidly. The first two were wide, but the next flung Shunkell around and toppled him down the rock face like a rag doll.

Jakaman could still have done something; he had a gun, and Halder was on his knees by the door, wounded but not dead.

Jakaman decided this was no place for him any more, and stuffed his gun under a loose rock. Shunkell was dead, and there was this one on the roof spraying lead all over the place, and more of them now rushing out into the garden. There was no profit in being a dead hero.

He began a hasty withdrawal, cautious at first, and then in a noisier fashion as his panic increased. There was more shooting, vaguely in his direction, which accelerated his progress and made him clumsier than he should have been. He fell headlong down the scrub several times, and his movements became wilder and less careful, so that a particularly rough landing twisted his ankle, and the search party picked him up before he got anywhere near the car.

When the time came later to surrender him to the lawful authorities, he was in a poor condition. He had damaged ribs and some of his teeth were with him no more. Halder's men had good reason not to handle him gently, although he was prepared to swear on his mother's grave that he had done none of the shooting. It helped him very little.

Without any undue pressure he indicated where the others could be found. He was in dire trouble himself, and they could take their share. If he ever got back to Sansovino he would tell a version of the incident at the villa which would show how gallant he alone had conducted himself; Halder had been shot and who was to say Jakaman had not done it? Shunkell was dead.

Accordingly a police contingent with plenty of hardware had swooped down on that remote farm, and the remainder were gathered in with no resistance. It would thus be some time before the catastrophic news reached Sansovino.

Tony Duchenne was finding it difficult to book himself a flight in the right direction.

There were vacancies on a morning flight to Jamaica, but Jamaica was the last place he intended to visit. There was a charter freight run west to Barbados and Trinidad, but he was unable to persuade the pilot to divert and drop him at Caracas, not even for a handsome consideration in cash.

He had to wait for a late afternoon flight to Caracas, which would probably mean spending a night there.

Every time he walked past Margolies' empty bungalow he could hear that police officer's crisp voice: *'You will come with me, Senor'*. And the warning about choosing his companions more carefully – very sound advice.

He had taken his seat in the aircraft when he saw Margolies arriving across the tarmac, and he was not alone; he was carrying a case, and the guards were on each side of him.

One of them pushed Margolies up into the aircraft and said, 'Do not come back.'

Margolies made no reply. He was un-shaven and dishevelled. He had no tie, his suit had clearly been slept in. He dropped into the vacant seat next to Tony.

'Welcome to freedom,' said Tony. 'Was it rough?'

'It was nothing,' said Margolies. 'I've seen the inside of better jails. Boy, do I stink.'

He pulled out his wallet. There was still some money there, a little, but his cigarette case and his lighter had gone.

Tony gave him a cigarette. They were airborne a few minutes later. Margolies took his remaining case back to the toilet, and when he returned he had shaved and changed his shirt and put on a tie.

'Tossed into jail and then deported, how's that for a score?' he said. 'I must be slipping.'

'The policeman who arrested you said something about bribing an engineer at the airport,' said Tony.

'A grease-monkey,' said Margolies. 'They must have seen us talking – or the young bastard shopped me. Morane is on the way to London now, with that guy Brockway. I would like to see that Morane in a concrete overcoat.'

'I know somebody else who feels the same way,' said Tony. 'He paid for my trip to Sansovino, and he'll be very interested to hear where Morane has gone.'

'Would I know him?'

'He used to be the boss at Sansovino. Morane kicked him out and murdered his wife and his son, and some of his friends.'

'Halder,' said Margolies. 'I heard of him. I thought he got liquidated in the revolution. Does he have any organisation going?'

'Not really,' said Tony. 'But his dearest wish is to put a bullet in Aloysius Morane.'

'And where do you come in?'

'I came to gather information,' said Tony. 'That's all. From what I know of Halder, he'll probably take off for England – in fact, I'm sure he will, and if he asks me to go with him I expect I will.'

'To do what?' said Margolies. 'You're no torpedo.'

'I understand Halder intends to do the job himself.'

'Crazy,' said Margolies. 'Is he serious?'

'Very. It's a personal vendetta.'

'He'll never make it on his own,' said Margolies. 'It needs a professional. I know a guy in England who'd do a good job, he's kind of retired, but he'd do it for the right fee, Bennie Lucas – if you mentioned I sent you.'

'I don't think Halder would like that,' said Tony. 'With him it's personal.'

'He'll never get near Morane,' said Margolies. 'Bennie Lucas knows his way around – and London isn't an easy place to work in, believe me. Bennie will give you a nice clean job with no backfire – hell, I'd be ready to put up half the money myself to get a hit done on Morane.'

'I'll suggest it,' said Tony. 'How do we get hold of this Bennie Lucas?'

'The last I heard,' said Margolies, 'he was running some kind of a building business. Bristol I think it was, some place like that. Anyway, we have this stopover at Caracas tonight and I'll do some checking on the phone, somebody will know, okay?'

'You must run quite an organisation yourself,' said Tony carefully.

'Just business,' said Clement Margolies. 'You lose a bit and you win a bit – Sansovino was a loss, so I have to even it up. How about something to drink?'

From Caracas that evening Tony tried to get a call through to the *Villa Hermosa*, but without success. Margolies did better after a number of calls. He gave Tony a slip of paper with some phone numbers in London and Bristol, and the names of saloons, also in London and Bristol, where Bennie Lucas might be contacted.

'He's still in business,' said Margolies. 'The story is that he made a sweet hit a coupla months back, in Morocco. But he's back in England now – you buy him and you'll be doing us all a big favour.'

'Including your associates in Miami?' said Tony, smiling. 'I don't suppose they're too happy about the way things turned out for you.'

Margolies didn't smile. He hunched his shoulders and for a moment his eyes were hard.

'Let's not talk about that,' he said.

He insisted on showing Tony the night life of Caracas. In some of the clubs, the more expensive ones, he was greeted as a very welcome visitor, with preferential service and drinks on the house. Tony found it an exhausting experience as the night pro-gressed, and would much rather have been in his hotel bedroom trying to catch up on his sleep.

In one of the more garish dives he was offered the company of a plump blonde in a see-through dress. He felt obliged to dance with her since Margolies was engaged in some kind of a business conversation with the manager, and the lady's approaches on the dance floor were embarrassingly in-decent, so that he politely declined her invi-tation to go upstairs and continue the process in more privacy and comfort. He would not be able to do her justice.

Later she tried it on with Margolies and he told her to go peddle it elsewhere and stuffed some dollar bills down the front of her dress, so she was not all that insulted.

Tony and Margolies separated that night. Margolies said he had some things to see to before he got a plane to Miami, and Tony's flight to Mexico City had an early take-off.

'I'll be expecting some news from London,' said Margolies. 'If you ever get to Miami be sure to look me up, you hear?'

'I hear,' said Tony.

'That Halder guy, you tell him from me he's too old to pull a trick like that on his own... I been in the business and I know what it takes.'

'You've convinced me,' said Tony. 'Tell me, what's the going rate for this kind of a job?'

Margolies stared at him hard for a moment, frosty hostility suddenly bright in his eyes.

'That a serious question? Sounded like you think it's some kind of a joke – arranging a hit isn't funny, Mister Duchenne.'

'I'm sorry if I sounded flippant,' said Tony. 'I didn't mean it.'

'That's okay then,' said Margolies, still fixing him with the cold and unfriendly stare. 'I wouldn't want to think I been wasting my time with you. I made an offer you won't get anywhere else.'

'I appreciate your efforts,' said Tony. Margolies was touchy, probably a matter of prestige – the professional giving the rank amateurs the benefit of his experience: how to arrange an assassination efficiently.

'I will pass the information on to Halder,' said Tony.

'It's confidential,' said Margolies. 'You tell him to think about it good and hard. Morane is surrounded by private muscle wherever he goes. It needs a good man to get him, and Bennie Lucas is very good. You meet his price and he'll give you a quality job.'

They were in Tony's bedroom. He had smoked too much and he had taken too many drinks. His head ached and he badly wanted to get to bed.

'Is Halder some kind of a nut?' said Margolies.

'He wants Morane dead,' said Tony.

'He must be loaded,' said Margolies.

'He is.'

'That figures,' said Margolies. 'He was the top man on that island for a long time, so

215

why hasn't Morane done anything about him?'

'He sent a gang of toughs to Acapulco, that's where Halder has been staying. When I left they hadn't done much, a little indiscriminate shooting, which I for one found most unpleasant.'

'You never pulled a gun on anybody in your life, right?'

'Very right,' said Tony. 'Guns scare me and I don't mind admitting it.'

'Keep it like that and you might live longer,' said Margolies. 'Leave the hardware to the guys who know how to use it, and that goes for Halder as well. Make a deal with Bennie Lucas and Morane is as good as dead – you'll never get better advice.'

'You could be right,' said Tony.

'Have a nice ride tomorrow,' said Margolies. He nodded a farewell, shook hands without another word, and walked smartly out of the room, a plump figure of a middle-aged man with nothing about him to suggest what he really was, which made him all the more dangerous. All the friendly façade could vanish in an instant when something happened that didn't suit his plans. And a 'hit' would be arranged. A business proposition. No fuss. A quality job done by an expert for the appropriate fee.

The flight to Mexico City the next morning was delayed for some two hours owing to a mechanical fault in the hydraulic system. The delay was prolonged, the fault proved obscure and difficult to trace, and there was no replacement aircraft available. They finally took off hours behind schedule and ran into a tropical storm over the sea which tossed them about very uncomfortably.

There was an emergency stop at San José since the hydraulics were still acting up, and the weary passengers could do nothing but complain and wait some more.

They reached Mexico City so late that Tony found it impossible to book himself on a night flight to Acapulco, so he reserved a seat on the first plane out in the morning and took a taxi to the hotel where he had stopped before. They had a vacancy. Not a luxury suite this time, just a room with a shower – and a telephone. He could also get some food.

But first he had to phone the villa. Ambrose Halder answered.

'Morane has gone to London,' said Tony. 'So I've come back – how is it all with you?'

And Ambrose Halder told him.

He sat on his bed for a very long time, stunned and not willing to believe what he had heard – she had even been buried that very afternoon…

The thought of having to spend a night in that room was intolerable. He went down to the reception desk and told them he had to have a car right away, he would drive it himself, to Acapulco, tonight.

And while he waited he would have the quickest meal they could serve. Coffee, no liquor. An emergency? It was. And he would pay for the room he hadn't occupied, of course.

In less than half an hour he was on the road, having parted with another notable portion of Halder's money, and in the savage mood that possessed him he was ready to get rid of every last dollar of that damn money to put an end to this miserable journey.

He had asked for a fast car and they had produced a blue Porsche that went like a bullet and hugged the road even on the steepest bends.

She was dead and it was Halder who should have died ... there was no justice in it.

11

'She loved you,' said Halder. 'I knew that when you left here, and she did not have to tell me, Tony Duchenne. I knew her so well, she was a very honest person.'

He had his right arm in a sling. Shunkell's second bullet had inflicted only a flesh wound along his forearm, missing the bone. He looked grey and much older.

'I wish I had died instead of her,' he said. 'That would have been fitting.'

'I think so, too,' said Tony.

'I am leaving this afternoon,' said Halder. 'They will be glad to see the back of me here officially. I will be in London tomorrow.'

'I'm coming with you,' said Tony, 'if you'll have me. I have a personal interest in this thing, just as you have, and you'll need me. With that arm you can't hope to do anything about Morane, so there's no point in following him to England unless you agree to have something arranged – you can't do it, and neither can I, but I can get in touch with the man who can.'

'It is not the way I wanted it,' said Halder. 'To hire somebody else to do my work.'

'You've no choice,' said Tony steadily, 'unless you want to forget the whole dirty business, in which case I'll go to London and see if I can meet whatever payment this Bennie Lucas wants – at least I'll find him and see what he thinks. Now I'll get Ernesto to show me where she is buried, and when I come back you tell me what you've decided.'

He stood alone by that slender mound of freshly dug earth; it had been heaped with flowers, the flowers she had loved and tended. He was filled with bitterness at the futility of it all, so much loveliness and warmth, all gone – and for what?

Ernesto drove him back to the villa in silence, but before he got out of the car Ernesto said softly, 'I wish to say this, Senor – for all my life I will be happy that I killed the man who did it, and for all my life I will be sad that I did not shoot first... I am nothing but a fool of a man.'

'You're all right with me, Ernesto,' said Tony. 'None better.'

'She was a fine lady,' said Ernesto. 'Now go with God, Senor.'

'It will be as you suggest,' said Halder. 'I have thought it over, and I agree with you.'

'Good,' said Tony. 'We will find Bennie Lucas and if he says it can't be done we'll both accept his expert opinion.'

'As you wish,' said Halder. 'We leave within the hour, I have made all the arrangements, and I will be happy to have you with me. Can you be ready to travel?'

'I'm ready now,' said Tony.

They left Acapulco in brilliant sunshine. They arrived in London in a summer drizzle. Rooms had been reserved in a quiet hotel in Kensington, and Ambrose Halder, suffering from jet-fatigue, had to rest for a while. Tony began to work on that list of pubs and phone numbers that Margolies had given him; it was a frustrating experience because nobody in any of the pubs would admit they had ever heard of Bennie Lucas, and some of the private numbers didn't answer at all.

He was nearly at the end of the list when he got through to one of the Bristol numbers, and a male voice said, 'Who wants him?'

'He doesn't know me,' said Tony, 'but we have a mutual friend in America.'

'That's nice. So?'

'If he's there I would very much like to speak to him.'

'You're doing that, chum. I'm Bennie Lucas. Who's the Yank you're talking about?'

'Clement Margolies – does the name ring a bell?'

There was a silence.

'It's about a business proposition,' said Tony. 'Margolies thought you might be interested, it would be worth your while. Could we meet somewhere soon?'

'How soon?'

'Tonight,' said Tony. 'I'm phoning from London, but I'm mobile.'

'No funny business?'

'No funny business,' said Tony. 'A straight business discussion – Margolies gave you a very strong recommendation, Mr Lucas.'

'I know about me, I'm wondering about you. There's a small bar in the station approach at Reading. I could be there in two hours. Give me a clue how I'll recognise you.'

'I'm a Canadian. I have a slight limp. I'll be wearing a summer-weight grey suit–'

'That's enough. Be alone. How was old Clem?'

'He was losing,' said Tony. 'You could say the proposition I have in mind was his idea.'

'Don't keep me waiting around.' Bennie Lucas cut the connection. Very businesslike, it inspired confidence.

Tony was there in good time. Halder had wanted to come with him, and Tony had pointed out that Lucas had made the condition, and if they both turned up he would probably decide they weren't to be trusted and have nothing more to do with the business.

There were plenty of patrons in the small bar because it was so handy for the mainline station. Tony got himself a 'Johnny Walker'. There was no room to sit, so he stood near the door, and he was being very careful not to make it too evident that he was waiting for anybody. The initial stages were bound to be delicate: they were hoping to hire a professional assassin for a specific task. An execution.

There was nobody in the bar who even remotely looked like his notion of a man who would kill for a fee. He finished his drink, his stomach was still suffering from the effects of the long haul across from Mexico, and he knew that another drink would be unwise. So he stood there with an empty glass.

A nondescript little man in a loose tweed

jacket pushed past him to the door and said softly, 'Outside'.

Tony followed him out and down the approach and into the street and the man didn't once look back. They went under the railway arch and into a car park, and there the man stopped and faced him.

Bennie Lucas was the kind of quiet man most people wouldn't remember a minute after he had passed them in the street. He was the man nobody ever had any reason to notice, and unless you were a trained observer you would be ready to swear that he hadn't been there at all.

He was about thirty-seven years old, of medium build, and very ordinary in his dress. He had thinning brown hair and sharp blue eyes, and a mild manner as though apologising for himself, which fooled some women into thinking he was lonely and in need of their loving care.

He had never married, and had never even been in the danger zone. There were occasions when he needed a woman, but she had to understand from the start that when it was over it was over. Very tidy and no unnecessary problems. Bennie's movements tended to be erratic at times, and any self-respecting wife likes to know just what the hell the breadwinner reckons he's up to when he pushes off without warning for days at a time and then won't explain where he has been. It also gets the neighbours talking.

'We'll drive around a bit and get acquainted,' said Bennie.

The car was a green Cortina. 'I drive and you talk,' said Bennie, 'and if I don't like what I hear, that's it for good.' He started the car and pulled out into the street. 'No obligation on either side, right?'

He drove through the streets and he went back on his tracks, taking sudden turnings, left and right, and watching in his mirror.

'It's all right,' said Tony. 'I haven't arranged for anybody to follow us. I'm on my own.'

'What do I know about you?' said Bennie. 'Nothing. So let me do my own worrying.'

It was a fair answer, in the circumstances. Why should Bennie trust a stranger? At length he said he was satisfied that nobody could be on their tail. On a piece of open ground near Sonning, he stopped the car and gave his passenger a long and silent inspection.

'Are you tied in with Margolies?'

'No,' said Tony. 'We met on a trip to an island in the Caribbean. We found we had things in common.'

'Let's hear about it,' said Bennie. 'Without prejudice, if I don't like it I'll tell you here and now and no harm done.'

Tony told him in enough detail to save too many questions, and Bennie listened with the polite attention of a professional man with a client. When Tony had finished, Bennie took out a battered case and offered Tony a cigarette.

'And you don't know where this bloke is staying?'

'No,' said Tony. 'It will be in London. One of the better hotels, I imagine. Morane will be anxious to make a good impression.'

'I will take a little look at the situation and tell you what I think.'

'We'd be grateful if you would.' So he wasn't turning it down flat. Tony felt easier.

'You'll have to be more than grateful,' said Bennie. 'There'll be the preliminary expenses, chum, before we get down to cases. I'll have to sweeten a few people. You with me?'

Tony nodded. 'How much?'

'I'll make a start tonight,' said Bennie. 'What's your cash position as of now?'

Tony took out his wallet. 'Sixty,' he said. 'We can have more by tomorrow morning.'

Bennie took the money. 'I'll ring your

hotel at midday; have four hundred in fivers; I'll tell you then where we meet. How long do we have?'

'I don't know,' said Tony. 'I don't know how long Morane will be over here.'

'I don't like rushing a job,' said Bennie. 'Makes for a sloppy operation. We'll have to see.'

He drove back into Reading at speed, and dropped Tony near the station.

'If you're driving up to London I could use a lift,' said Tony. 'I came down by train.'

'Sorry,' said Bennie. 'I make it a rule never to socialise at this stage, it's safer that way if I find the job isn't on, see what I mean?'

Tony thought that was carrying caution to excess, but he didn't say so.

'Four hundred, twelve o'clock tomorrow. I may have something for you.' Bennie drove off, and Tony went up into the station. He had to wait some time for a train, and there was another wait at Paddington for a taxi.

Ambrose Halder was up, in dressing-gown and pyjamas. The hotel had sent a doctor to renew the dressing on Halder's arm, and the doctor had advised him to spend a few days in bed, advice which Halder was likely to ignore.

'I think he's the right man for us,' said Tony. 'Very competent and sharp in an unobtrusive way, not the kind of man to make any mistakes.'

'He is in a line of business where mistakes cannot be afforded,' said Halder. 'I would like to meet him tomorrow.'

Bennie Lucas drove into Brixton, into streets of houses that had come down in the world, where there were almost more coloureds than whites, where nobody would notice his comings and his goings, as long as he paid his rent. He was such an ordinary little man, clearly not prosperous, and not likely to cause any disturbance.

After making a few calls he found what he wanted, a furnished room in a house that was let off to tenants who wouldn't be staying too long and thus wouldn't be too fussy. The landlord was an amiable Jamaican who lived in the basement with a white girl. Zekiel Thomas was a skinny character with an everlasting grin and a ready hand out for his rent in advance and no references required.

Bennie paid for two weeks, including a bit extra for the television, and the use of a transistor set. The room was on the first floor, in the front. Opposite there was a hoarding with some planks missing, and a derelict area where the developers had made a start. It was not the liveliest of views.

Bennie had brought only a small case with him. The important part of his luggage was in the boot of the Cortina, secured by a special lock that would defy any prowling sneak-thief – it would take a craftsman to force it open, and a craftsman does not go about trying to bust the boot of a car, unless it is something promising like a Rolls not a three-year-old Cortina with dented wings.

There was a gas ring in the room, but Zekiel pointed out that officially real cooking was not allowed in the rooms, and Bennie said that was okay because he would be eating out. Zekiel gave him a key to the front door, flashed his teeth again, and shambled off.

Bennie unpacked his small case so as to make it look all right if that grinning ape came sniffing around when he was out. He had just a few clothes, they wouldn't tell anybody anything about him except that he bought his stuff where everybody bought it. Zekiel hadn't asked him what he did for his bread and he hadn't volunteered any information. They both knew he was paying over the odds for the room.

On his way down he met a woman who had just come in, and he stood aside to let her come up the stairs. She gave him a smile and a murmured thank you. Not a bad-looking piece. Tall – Bennie preferred them tall, being only middle size himself. Good legs and blonde hair and big breasts – another of Bennie's private preferences. She was no chicken but she wasn't about to fall apart.

So he said good evening. You never could tell – there might be some spare time. He looked back halfway down the stairs and she was unlocking a door across the landing from his. Convenient. And he thought she paused before she went in and glanced down at him.

He found a telephone kiosk that was still in working order, which was rare in that neighbourhood. He made a list of the possible hotels in the West End, not a long list because Morane would want to be well accommodated. He put the same question each time: had Mr Aloysius Morane booked in yet? The first five hotels had never heard of the gentleman.

He ran out of change. There was a club

nearby, full of noise and bouncing bodies. Nobody questioned him, he bought a bottle of gin and some bitter lemon, and collected enough change to finish his job, even if it took all night.

Number eleven gave him what he was after: Mr Morane was a guest at the hotel but he was out dining with friends, and was there any message?

Bennie said thanks very much and he would try again in the morning. He walked back to his lodgings, happy with himself. The Pavilion Court Hotel, he would take a nice long look at it in the morning. Not an easy place to check, but better than some of the more celebrated hotels.

He was getting to the top of the stairs when a door on the landing opened, and he knew it was the bathroom. The woman he had met was coming out, and she stood there with the light behind her for a moment; she wore a thin wrap, it was as good as transparent, and it made her legs look very nice all the way up. She put the light out as he came up, and she didn't scuttle across to her room.

'We're neighbours,' said Bennie. 'I'm Bennie Lucas.' He held out his hand and the package of booze chinked. There was a nice scented bathroom smell about her as she gave him her hand.

'Dorothy Collins,' she said. 'I'm glad to meet you Mr Lucas. I hope you'll be comfortable here.'

'I'm sure I will,' he said, and neither of them made any move. She held the front of her wrap together with one hand, and the other smoothed her hair. She moistened her lips. She was interested. And Bennie was being so deferential and polite.

'Well,' she said, 'it's getting late–'

Still she didn't move the few steps to her own door. She had smoothed her hair to her satisfaction, and she knew she wasn't showing anything she shouldn't show. Not that she had anything to be ashamed of. He looked rather nice; just the right age.

'I was wondering,' he said diffidently, 'would you care to join me in a drink, Miss Collins? Sort of a night-cap?'

'I shouldn't,' she said. 'I mean, I don't know you–'

'Nothing like a little drink to get acquainted,' said Bennie. 'Please.'

'I bet you don't have any glasses,' she said, smiling, and he knew he had started. 'I'll bring some, give me a couple of minutes – just one little drink, mind you.'

When she appeared in his room she had a

tray with two glasses and a plate with some biscuits. She had done her face and she had tied the sash of her wrap, but that was all she wore.

He took the glasses from her. 'I hope gin and bitter lemon is okay,' he said. 'It's all I have at the moment.'

'Not too much bitter lemon,' she said. 'Don't kill the gin.'

That sounded promising. There was only one armchair and she had it, tucking the folds of her wrap around her legs. He poured a drink that was two-thirds gin.

'Cheers,' she said, and dealt with it like tap water. 'And what brings you to this part of town, Mr Lucas?'

'Business,' he said. 'I'm a travelling rep. Hardware and sundries. Very dull.'

She told him she worked as a cashier in a neighbouring supermarket. She had been married once, to a radio officer in the Merchant Navy, but after a couple of years the bastard had ditched her, and the last she had heard about him he had taken some shore job in Hong Kong; she thought he had probably shacked up with one of those slant-eyed bitches. And not a penny out of him. So she had shed him officially.

Bennie agreed that it was rough.

'That's life,' said Dorothy. 'I can't pretend I don't miss having a man around the place … know what I mean?'

'I've never been married,' said Bennie, 'but I know what you mean. It's a lousy life for most of us.'

He kept pouring the gin for her, and now it was nearly neat. She was loosening up quickly. She wasn't so bothered about that wrap when it slid open and he saw most of what she had. It was months since he'd had a woman, and this one was ready for it.

Her eyes were bright and her mouth was pouty and she was showing the tip of her tongue whenever he bent over her to refill her glass. When he stroked the back of her neck she leaned back and laughed softly up into his face.

He eased the wrap off one of her shoulders, and a large firm breast was on view.

'Saucy,' she murmured. 'Whatever next?'

'Watch this space,' he said. Dorothy Collins was coming to the boil.

She put her glass on the floor by her chair and shrugged the wrap completely free down to her waist.

'If you're interested,' she said, 'that's the set.'

'I won't be shouting for help,' he said.

'It's a funny thing,' she said. 'Here I am sitting bloody near starkers in front of you and I only met you just now.'

'What's the problem?' said Bennie.

He locked the door and began to undress, folding his clothes tidily away. Why rush? Dorothy wasn't going anywhere, was she?

She had undone her wrap and it lay on the floor. She sat on the side of the bed.

'I'll have another little drink to give me strength,' she said. He didn't look much in his clothes, but without them he was equipped like a stallion, plenty in the place where it counted.

'Just don't get yourself stoned,' he said, making her a moderate drink this time. 'I like a woman to know what's happening when she is in bed with me.'

She had stacked the pillows behind her, and she was occupying most of the single bed, but she shifted over to make room for him as he let her finish the gin.

'Listen,' she said chattily, 'I hope you don't think I do this regularly.'

'We haven't done anything yet,' he said. He gazed at the undulating expanse of her lush body, and then at her expectant face. 'If you want to change your mind it's a bit late for that.'

'You do like me a little bit, don't you?' she said. 'You really haven't said a nice thing to me yet–'

'Do we talk all night or do we get some action?' he said. He whipped the pillows away and let her sink back on to the bed.

Dorothy Collins was a healthy normal woman, and she quite liked a bit of rough stuff in bed, but this Bennie with the cold blue eyes was something right out of her considerable experience. It was fun at first, sort of exciting, being pushed about like that, but it went on too long and he was too violent. It became an exercise in sexual techniques, regardless of her protests that she'd had enough, really enough. He was frightening her, and there was no loving in it, none of the tenderness a woman has the right to expect from the man in bed with her.

And the only words he was using were not nice ones. When he had finished with her he lay on the bed and watched her wriggle un-steadily into her wrap. Her face was flushed and her mouth was swollen and she didn't want to look at him.

'You were okay,' he said. 'Don't look so sorry for yourself – you were okay, I mean that.'

'You're a swine and I mean that as well,' she said.

'We'll go better next time,' he said. 'You need to loosen up a bit.'

'There won't be a next time.'

His laugh followed her as she padded across the room. She slammed the door. The bed smelt of her, and he wished he had some fresh sheets. He felt easy and relaxed. There was no doubt about it, as an occasional piece of therapy, a bundle with a woman with big boobs paid a dividend. And you didn't even have to like the woman, anyone would do, more or less. He had just proved that. Right?

She'd be around for some more. Women in her age group were gluttons for punishment. Take Bennie's word for it.

12

They were on the grass slope across from the ornamental water, in the park, by the Bayswater Road entrance. There were plenty of people about in the lunch-time sunshine, and Halder was in the only chair they could get. Tony Duchenne sat on the grass with Bennie Lucas, three men just chatting together, the old one with his arm in a sling.

Bennie had arrived late at the meeting place, and he hadn't bothered to apologise because he had been busy on their account and he was operating single-handed on a job that needed a team.

'Morane has a suite on the second floor,' he said. 'He has a bloke with him all the time, a strong-arm character. When he travels he uses a chauffeur-driven car and the bloke sits with the driver. They're in the city now, London Wall, with the banking outfit, they'll be there all day. That's as far as I've got. He booked for a week at the hotel.'

'Do you think it's going to be possible?' said Halder.

'Kennedy got it,' said Bennie. 'But that was in Dallas. Even now nobody knows for sure how it was fixed. It takes an organisation, and we don't have an organisation.'

'But can it be done?' Halder said softly.

Bennie chewed a stem of grass. 'It can. It may be tricky.'

'I will pay five thousand pounds,' said Halder.

Bennie was looking at Tony Duchenne. He'd already had the four hundred, it was in his pocket, and he had refused to say a word until it had been handed over.

'I said five thousand,' Halder repeated.

'I heard you,' said Bennie.

'Well?'

'He's worth more than that to you,' said Bennie.

'I'll double it,' said Halder, and he sounded weary. 'If that doesn't suit you we'll forget we ever saw you.'

'I take the risk,' said Bennie, 'so I name the price. Ten is okay.'

'Thank you.' Halder got up stiffly. 'I will leave you two to arrange any further details.' He walked off, picking his way fastidiously among the couples sprawling on the grass.

'That's a funny bloke,' said Bennie. 'Kind of high-handed.'

'It's his money,' said Tony.

'Very touchy,' said Bennie.

'For ten thousand he has the right to be a little more than touchy,' said Tony. 'What's the next move?'

'Information,' said Bennie. 'I have to know a lot more about Morane's movements. I'll tell you one thing I won't be doing – I won't bash my way into the hotel on the off chance of getting a shot at him and his bodyguard, I don't work that way – that needs a back-up team inside and outside the building, especially outside with a fast car, and you need one hell of a slice of luck.'

'Don't look at me,' said Tony. 'I'm not your man. I'm in the audience. You have my very best wishes.'

Bennie rolled over on his stomach and nibbled some more grass. 'It looks easy on the telly,' he said, 'following a car around, nobody ever spots it, nobody ever gets in the way, and there's always somewhere to park with no double yellow lines.'

'Very fraught,' said Tony. 'How do we get in touch with you?'

'You don't,' said Bennie. 'I'll call you when I have to. I'll be moving around and I don't know where I'll fetch up. So I'll want one of you on tap at your hotel.'

'We'll arrange it,' said Tony.

'Morane might change his plans,' said Bennie. 'He's after big money, and that can take time – on the other hand he might get a flat refusal and be on the way home tomorrow. As I told you, it could be tricky, and I never hurry a job – that's the only way to stay out of jail.'

Tony took the point. There was a nice family having a picnic nearby, mum and dad on a rug with the fodder, and a brace of pleasant little kids knocking a coloured ball around. While he and Bennie Lucas discussed a safe way of killing.

'I gather Margolies thought he had a deal all tied up with Morane,' said Tony. 'Some kind of a big development racket, and at the last moment Morane elbowed him out.'

Bennie spat out some chewed grass. 'Boy, I bet that riled him. Clem Margolies wouldn't like that.'

'He didn't,' said Tony. 'That was why he gave me your name. Is he one of the Mafia bosses? That was the impression I got.'

Bennie sat up straight. 'He has a lot of interests. If Morane ever visited Miami he wouldn't be needing any return ticket.'

'We must hope he doesn't find London any safer,' said Tony.

'You won't expect me to take him out on a crowded street,' said Bennie.

'We leave the method to you,' said Tony. The coloured ball landed between them and Tony bounced it back to the kids, and the mother said thank you.

'He won't be working all day and all night,' said Bennie. 'He'll have to relax some time. What about women? He's a long way from home and there are plenty of birds around.'

'I didn't hear anything about his private life while I was on the island,' said Tony. 'The locals weren't inclined to gossip about him, at least not to me.'

'There's a lot of home-work to be done before it's set up the way I like it, and we don't know how much time we have. You can tell that old bloke he can start collecting my fee – we might be in business sooner than we expect.' Bennie got up, brushed the loose grass from his clothes, and walked off towards the Bayswater Road exit. A professional killer picking his way politely around the peaceful citizens lazing on the grass, an insignificant man and not worth a second glance.

Tony waited there on the grass for a while. He found himself envying that married couple with their two lively kids playing in the sunshine; then he noticed that the father was giving full attention to a girl who was squatting with her knees up and showing her thighs right to the junction and a snippet of blue briefs, just a few yards away.

His wife muttered something at him, and Tony heard him tell her to mind her own bloody business. Another sad glimpse of the frailty of the married condition.

He left the park and had a beer and a sandwich in a pub where the customers could sit outside on a piece of chequered pavement and watch the traffic. It was a pub he remembered from his days as a student in London; it had seemed brighter then, especially on a summer evening when he would have a girl with him, one of the many girls of those carefree days, with all the world waiting for them, and life that would go on for ever.

The girls would be married now, most of them divorced as well.

He rang the hotel. 'I think Bennie Lucas is our man,' he said.

'I was not impressed,' said Halder.

'He knows his business,' said Tony. 'You can't do it, and I wouldn't even try. He wants one of us to be available on the phone all the time.'

'I will be here,' said Halder. 'I am not feeling energetic this afternoon.'

'Your arm must be bothering you,' said Tony. 'You ought to rest it, as the doctor suggested. We must at least give Bennie Lucas a chance to earn his money.'

'The money is of no great importance,' said Halder. 'I am buying a man to do what I would prefer to be doing myself. You will not expect me to be enthusiastic.'

'It's the best we can do,' said Tony. 'Or we can agree to let Morane soldier on until somebody else puts an end to him.'

Halder had put the phone down. Tony wandered down towards Marble Arch. This was an area he used to know. The traffic was a lot heavier now than when he whipped through it in his MGB hard-top. He turned into the cobbled mews where he had rented a flat over a garage. It all looked much the same, cars parked all along, window-boxes, and the pub on the top corner. The properties were smarter than he remembered, and the flat he had lived in had been recently painted and a balcony added over the front door. He guessed he couldn't afford to live there now if he had to buy it. And the cars were of a better quality.

A girl came out of the door at the far end

of the mews. She wore a dark blue trouser suit and she carried a shopping basket; she had long blonde hair and a tall slender figure.

She stopped when she saw him. 'It's Tony Duchenne, isn't it?' she said. 'My God, it *is* you!'

'Hullo, Jill,' he said. 'You look as elegant as ever. How are you?'

'I manage,' she said. 'It must be all of four years since I saw you last – I didn't even know you were in this country.'

'Just visiting,' he said.

'Let's not stand out here yapping,' she said. 'Come on in, the shopping can wait.'

'I'll come shopping with you,' he said.

'To hell with that,' she said. Then she noticed his limp. 'What happened to your leg?'

'A minor accident,' he said.

'You fell out of somebody's bed?' she said.

'You don't change,' he said, smiling at her. 'Always the happy phrase. Did you get married after all? I never heard.'

'How would you hear?' she said. 'You just vanished. My marital history is short and not sweet – we got married, and I booted him out two years ago.'

They went up the stairs he remembered so

clearly, and into the long narrow sitting-room where there had been so many memorable parties; it looked shabby now; the furniture and the carpets were worn and faded.

Jill Orchard threw her shopping basket into a corner, and turned to inspect him.

'Flourishing, evidently,' she said. 'Where have you been, Tony? I like your expensive tan.'

'The West Indies mostly,' he said.

'Lucky you. You're married of course?'

'Not so as you would notice,' he said. 'It didn't work.'

'That has a familiar ring,' she said. 'We are the divorcing generation. And now you're on the loose in London town.'

'Not quite,' he said. 'I'm over here on business.'

She was pouring drinks from a decanter. 'Draught sherry wine, the man called it,' she said. 'It's terrible but it's cheap and it's all I have in the place.'

Tony tried it cautiously. She was right. It was pretty bad. They sat and looked at each other. Old friends who didn't know where to start.

Jill gave him her lopsided grin and indicated the room. 'We had some fun here in the old days, you wouldn't think it now, would you?'

'I bet you still find plenty to keep you amused,' he said.

'My lease is up next month,' she said, 'and I can't afford to keep it on. I'm not really sorry – the fun has evaporated, and a genteel bed-sitter is more in my line now. I am a sober working girl.'

'The mind boggles,' he said. 'The Jill Orchard I knew was seldom sober and almost never at work. You mean you have a job?'

'Part-time,' she said. 'A boutique that suffers from the cash-flow shortage. The last refuge of the girl with little ability and an expensive education – and no rich papa behind her.'

He was remembering her background, both of her parents were dead and she had been brought up by an aunt.

'What about that wealthy aunt with the estate in the country?' he said. 'You took me down there for a week-end one... Wryton Place, that was its name–'

'Aunt Rosie,' said Jill, grinning, 'she thought I might marry you, the poor old trout was never really with it. She's damn nearly bankrupt now, so if you know of anybody who needs a snug Berkshire property in a very desirable location, Aunt Rosie would be happy to meet him.'

'How did she lose her money?' said Tony. 'I thought she had plenty, I can remember that she lived in some style.'

'She had an income from investments left her by her husband; he was on the Baltic Exchange, Uncle Freddie. She was a widow for about ten years, living quite comfortably – that was when you met her. Then she got the crazy idea that she could increase her income by playing the market – everybody was doing it and making a packet, on paper. Her solicitor tried to stop her, and her bank manager had fits when he realised what she was up to, even I had a dig at her, but it didn't make any difference. She got herself into a terrible tangle with some bogus firm who promised her all kinds of quick profits. You know how they operate with a rich widow, and Aunt Rosie was easy pickings for them. You can guess the ending – she just keeps herself afloat. Next year I expect she'll go under. Hell, what a tale of woe I've unloaded on you – you don't have to drink that sludge, Tony, I'll make us some coffee.'

She went into the kitchen and left the door open so that they could still talk.

'Are you going to be over here for long?' she said.

'Not long,' he said.

'You'll be looking up some of the old crowd? There are still a few of them around.'

'I might, if I have the time.'

'What's your job, Tony?'

'Political, after a fashion,' he said.

'That sounds important,' she said. 'Nobody heard a word from you after you left.'

'Wanderlust,' he said. 'I had itchy feet.'

She brought in the tray with the coffee. 'I have to work a split shift this evening,' she said. 'This is the night we keep open late, otherwise I might invite myself to dinner with you, which shows you what a little lady I am.'

'I'll give you a ring and we'll fix something up,' he said.

'Do that,' she said, and the expression on her face made it clear she didn't expect to hear from him again.

'You look like a man with no serious problems,' she said. 'You have everything in your life under control, and I'm happy for you, Tony.'

'I wish you were right,' he said.

'Your wife must have been a silly cow to let you go, or is that the wrong thing to say?'

'She was entitled to a mistake,' he said. 'I was hers. It doesn't much matter now.'

'We must have a good cry together some time,' she said cheerfully, 'amid the debris of our abandoned marriage beds. We should have something in common.'

She gave him a very direct look. 'I quite fancied you at one time, Tony.'

'It was mutual,' he said.

He was rescued by her phone ringing. She excused herself and went out into the hall at the top of the stairs, leaving the door ajar. So he had to hear. Her voice dropped into the soft intimate tone of a woman speaking to a man who is more than just another man on the phone. His name was Charles, and it appeared he wanted to come round then and there. There were some whispered bits that Tony couldn't hear, laughing protests, and then: 'Don't make it too early, sweetie … working, you know…'

So Jill Orchard was getting her share. And why not? She was easy to be with and she had her own place. Tony was recollecting her husband – an accountant, nuts about cricket and rugby, unhappy without a pint tankard in his fist; one of the boys, and slow to pay his round in the pub, thick as they come. Why the hell did people marry people?

He left shortly afterwards, and Jill came with him to do that shopping. The last he saw of her she was at the fish shop, pricing the kippers, and he hoped Charles liked kippers for supper.

In Bennie's line of business patience was of the first importance, because the surest way to ruin an operation was to rush it. You had to wait until it all added up right, and then you had to back your own judgment. Bennie always worked solo. He trusted nobody but himself, and one man can move around without attracting attention if he knows his business.

He had followed Morane and the guard back from the City late in the afternoon to the hotel, through the thick traffic, which was in itself no mean effort. Morane had vanished into the hotel with his escort, and the chauffeur had driven the car round to the rear of the hotel.

Bennie had made his reconnaissance the day before, and he knew the car Morane had been using was supplied by the hotel. The main entrance to the Pavilion Court had a handsome portico, curving in off the wide street, and there was always a porter on duty – in a green uniform with gold braid and white gloves, and Bennie was being very careful not to be noticed by him.

He wandered down the slope to the rear of the building. The chauffeur was hosing the car down, and Bennie, an interested on-looker, said he was making a good job of it, which got them chatting. It was easy after that for Bennie to coax the conversation the way he wanted it to go. The chauffeur was off duty for the rest of the evening – there was a Rolls coming to pick up the bloke he'd been ferrying about.

'A Rolls?' said Bennie. 'Sounds like some-body's got money all right.'

'The bankers have got it all, matey, not blokes like you and me.' The chauffeur parked the car inside the main covered garage, got into a maroon Anglia, and drove off.

Just before eight o'clock that evening Bennie saw the Rolls arriving under the portico, and the porter sprang into action almost before it had stopped. There was a uniformed chauffeur, and a man in a dinner jacket emerged from the back seat, nodded at the porter, and went into the hotel.

Bennie had been obliged to leave his car some distance away, but he had made a discreet investment in a taxi which waited nearby, and at a sign from Bennie the taxi driver had started his engine. It was not an ideal arrangement, but Bennie had to be ready to be mobile, and the driver had showed little curiosity once he saw the colour of Bennie's money, and Bennie wasn't carrying any package so he wasn't one of those bomb-throwing terrorists. Bennie had told him it was a commercial job he was on, trade secrets, that kind of lark, and they would just be following the Rolls, nothing more.

In the shoulder holster which had been tailored to his requirements Bennie had the .25 Beretta, not his favourite weapon.

The two men came out of the hotel, Morane also dressed for dinner, but his guard wasn't with him. Bennie climbed into his taxi.

'That's it,' he said.

A Rolls-Royce is not the most difficult of vehicles to follow, since they are not all that thick on the ground even in the West End, and this one was being driven at a dignified pace. It was a short ride. Morane could have walked it with ease. In which case Bennie might have attended to him.

The Rolls stopped by an imposing building near Hyde Park Corner, the taxi ran along and slowed a little.

'I can't wait here,' said the driver. 'That's Sir Geoffrey Miller's place they went in – they reckon he's a millionaire, got his own bank, something like that.'

'Nice,' said Bennie.

The Rolls went purring past, only the chauffeur in it. Sir Geoffrey Miller was entertaining Morane to dinner, that was clear. Bennie had his taxi take him back to where they had started, and paid the driver off handsomely.

He collected his car and spent some time circling the Hyde Park area, which proved to be a tedious business after the first hour. He allowed himself a brief respite for a cup of coffee and a sausage roll near a taxi stand, where he fitted into the background very easily.

It was a boring caper, but he was prepared to stay with it all night. It was around eleven o'clock when he next sighted the Rolls, pulling away from the house, and this time Bennie was facing the wrong way and he couldn't make a turn just there because of the oncoming traffic. The result was that he arrived back at the hotel as the Rolls was leaving, and the night porter stood under the portico, ready to repel the undesirables.

Bennie drove back to his lodgings. He had

arranged with a builder who had a small yard to park his car there at night; the yard was locked and Bennie had a key; to leave the car on the roadside regularly at night would be inviting trouble – some light-fingered bastard would happen along one night and nick it and leave him without transport, and without his gear, and the gear was important – without it he was nobody. This time he brought the bag in with him.

In his room he unpacked the bag, and once more took out the components that would assemble into his collapsible rifle. It was a Belgian job, very special and very expensive, with a telescopic sight. Each part had been separately wrapped so that the bag could be handled silently no matter how it was bumped around. With this gun Bennie Lucas would guarantee not to miss, given the right conditions, and if the conditions weren't right he never used it.

He oiled and wiped and checked all the moving parts; he assembled the gun and noted his time – as fast as ever. *Snip-snip-snip* – bang on target.

He took the gun apart and repacked the bag. Quietly he moved his bed out, lifted the carpet, and prised up the boards he had already loosened. The bag fitted the cavity snugly, and he put everything back the way it had been.

In her room across the landing Dorothy Collins had noted his return. She had been careful not to meet him again after the rotten way he had treated her that night. She still had the bruises on her thighs and elsewhere, and some memories about that episode that wouldn't leave her. Disgusting, really. It was like going to see one of those dirty sex films and seeing yourself in a leading part. Nasty and degrading. And now she just couldn't stop thinking about it.

It was worse when she was in bed, alone, and her mind and body started to act up as though he was there with her, doing all those things over again.

Sort of thrilling in a horrible way. And it was ruining her sleep. He was just a few steps across the landing. Surely he must think of her some time?

Just suppose he knocked on her door? She lay awake for a long time, waiting and listening. Willing him to come. But he didn't.

13

The following morning Bennie Lucas noticed an interesting variation in the pattern of Aloysius Morane's movements. For the first time there was no visit to the City. Accompanied by his bodyguard, Morane went shopping in Knightsbridge by taxi, and returned to the Pavilion Court Hotel with a number of parcels, and Bennie could only surmise that he was replenishing his wardrobe, which might mean that his mission in London was over.

So unless something handy took place, Bennie might be kissing himself good-bye to ten thousand nice big ones. He had picked up a few hundred quid for a little light exercise, mostly watching the hotel. Maybe this was going to be a non-starter. You couldn't expect to pull off a hit every time, even when you were as expert as Bennie knew he was. London in daylight was tricky.

In the afternoon Sir Geoffrey Miller's Rolls-Royce slid elegantly under the hotel portico;

there was the uniformed chauffeur, and a young feller in tweeds who went into the hotel. This time Bennie was not going to be caught short – if that Rolls was giving Morane a lift to the airport Bennie was going to be right there behind it, then he could phone Duchenne and the old bloke and tell them it had all fouled up.

He collected his green Cortina. He stopped slap in front of a *No Parking At Any Time* notice, opened his bonnet, and did the stranded driver bit, fiddling with his engine. No warden arrived to harass him.

Luggage was now being brought out to the Rolls. Morane and the young bloke got into the back, and the bodyguard saw them off from the steps of the hotel.

It had to be the airport, and Bennie settled down to keeping a discreet distance behind. He had no crazy ideas about pulling up alongside the Rolls and trying a quick blast at Morane through the window, not in these traffic conditions and operating solo. Furthermore, the Rolls was now bundling along at a fair lick, and Bennie was being kept busy not losing touch.

He was surprised when they sailed past the turn-off to the airport, and on through Slough and Maidenhead. They were heading out into the country, and no dawdling about it. If Morane was leaving he was taking an unusual route, and Bennie began to suspect that he had guessed wrong: Morane wasn't on the way out.

Bennie felt better. He just might manage a hit after all, given reasonable road conditions – if he could jockey that bloody great Rolls off the road when there was nothing else around. It was a slim prospect, and it would need a bit of luck – and it was not Bennie's habit to risk his neck on luck. All the same, he would stay with it and see.

Just beyond Henley the Rolls swung off the main road, and Bennie thought this might be his chance to move up closer, although there was still plenty of traffic about. Bennie reckoned himself an expert behind the wheel of a car, and on more than one fraught occasion he had owed his continuing liberty to his skill and judgement where there didn't seem room for a vehicle at speed.

But on those occasions he had always done a preliminary survey of the territory and knew what was around the next corner. This was different, he didn't know these roads, whereas the driver of the Rolls evidently knew them very well from the saucy way he was pushing that heavy car along, and

Bennie didn't think he had a hope in hell of getting close enough to do anything.

This was a high-priced neighbourhood; this was no gin-and-Jag slice of the commuter belt; there was real money all around here; big properties for the big people, like Sir Geoffrey Miller, for instance.

Bennie thought he had lost the Rolls, and he arrived just in time to see it turning in past some gates set in a lofty brick wall, the entrance to an estate where he couldn't follow because there was a bloke there ready to shut the gates behind the Rolls.

He drove along a little way and then went back on foot. The gates had some fancy gilded work, and he could pick out the name: *River Bank House*. There was a lodge and some shrubbery and a drive, but the house was out of sight.

Bennie went back to the Cortina and took a long look at the wall. It bordered the road as far as he could see, and it was in good condition; he was no acrobat, but he thought he could manage it, if he had to, but not yet and in broad daylight.

He traced the wall along to where the estate apparently ended; the wall went in among some trees, and there were fields and cows; the river couldn't be far away.

Half a mile farther on he came on the village, Datchford. Picture postcard stuff. A village green with the cricket square roped off in the middle; a few cottages that were too smart to be farm-workers' dwellings any longer; the pub was the Datchford Arms, with tubs of flowers along the front, and a framed menu by the main door with prices that took it right out of the class of a country pub.

Outside the one and only shop there was a telephone kiosk. Bennie checked the directory and verified what he had guessed: Sir Geoffrey Miller lived at *River Bank House*.

He put in a call to London. Aloysius Morane as a guest in a country house was a much better proposition than he had been in a hotel in the West End.

Tony Duchenne took the call.

'Datchford?' he said. 'I know the place. Very quaint. I used to visit a house near there, I remember the pub.'

'The Datchford Arms,' said Bennie. 'I'm looking right at it.'

'So he's a house-guest with Sir Geoffrey,' said Tony. 'I wonder how long he'll stay?'

'He bought some new clothes this morning,' said Bennie. 'He left that bodyguard behind, but there was a load of luggage – I don't fancy he's just there for the night.'

'That's good,' said Tony, 'isn't it?'

'It's improving,' said Bennie. 'Has that old man got the cash?'

'It's ready.'

'I'll be in touch.' Bennie rang off.

Ambrose Halder had been resting in his room; he was spending a lot of time doing just that while they waited; he was in a depressed mood, and Tony was finding him something of a trial.

He had been nursing his vengeance so long that he could think of little else, which made him poor company, and Tony wondered what he would have left once Morane had been accounted for – what point would there be left in his life?

A killing done by somebody else strictly for cash. That was a poor solution. Quite apart from being a crime. And Tony himself was an accessory before the fact, so he couldn't pretend that his hands were going to be clean.

More than once he was wishing he had never heard of the *Villa Hermosa* – and Clara? There had been enough killing, surely. He couldn't throw off all of his background and upbringing – murder was murder, no matter what excuse you gave yourself.

Lying on his bed, Ambrose Halder was not impressed when Tony tried to put his ideas into words.

'We are different kinds of people,' he said. 'You still have a life to live. Mine is over.'

'You've got years left,' said Tony.

'I have as little as I choose to have,' said Halder, getting off the bed. 'You wish to be no further implicated. Very well – I absolve you.'

'You're obsessed,' said Tony. 'Having Morane killed won't solve anything, will it?'

'You spoke and thought differently at Acapulco,' said Halder very softly. 'You have a tender conscience, Mr Duchenne, and a short memory – I have neither.'

'You intend to go on with this?' said Tony.

Halder smiled. 'Unless you feel it your duty to go to the police and have it stopped. They would be lenient with you if you turned Queen's evidence.'

Tony stared at him as he struggled to get into his jacket with his wounded arm still in a sling.

'I resent that,' he said.

'You are not being consistent,' said Halder, and made for the door into the sitting-room they shared.

Tony followed him out. 'What are you going to do now?'

'I am going to this village,' said Halder, 'Datchford. Where else would I go?'

'Bennie Lucas won't want you there,' said Tony. 'You'll only be in the way.'

'If I pay the piper, I call the tune,' said Halder.

'You don't keep a dog and bark yourself,' said Tony. 'How are you going to get there? It's right out in the country.'

'I will hire a car with a driver.'

Tony shook his head. 'Lucas won't like that, bringing a stranger on to the scene. You can't drive, if you arrive with a stranger Lucas won't do anything, you can be sure of that.'

He sat and drew the phone towards him. He caught Halder's eye. 'Not the police,' he said. 'I'm booking rooms at the Datchford Arms. You'll need some sort of a base down there, and so will Bennie Lucas. Does that make sense?'

Halder nodded.

'I used to know a girl, Jill Orchard,' said Tony. 'I ran into her only the other day. She had an aunt with a house in that neighbourhood, and I know where *River Bank House* is–'

'You are being inconsistent again,' said Halder.

'I need my head examining,' said Tony. 'Perhaps we both do.'

Bennie followed the wall along through the trees, away from the road; there were the fields on his right with the cows and now they were drifting across the grass to a field gate, it was milking time, and a small boy sat on the gate with a stick. He was in charge. So Bennie squatted down behind a bush until the cows had all gone through.

Presently he could see the shining curves of the river beyond the water meadows. Then over the wall the cluster of chimneys and roofs and some of the attic windows of the house. He had to climb a tree to get a sight of the house itself.

Bennie was no judge of architecture, but he thought this looked pretty nice. It had been there a long time and plenty of money had been spent on keeping it right. It faced south and the windows glinted in the sun. There was a terrace and flower beds and a long stretch of lawn at different levels right down to the water. He could see a landing stage and what had to be the boat-house alongside the edge of the water.

Getting inside there was going to be a doddle. They were taking tea on the terrace, half a dozen people, and he had no trouble in picking out Aloysius Morane in a light grey suit that Bennie had never seen him in before. A very upper-class tea party.

Two women, one young and one not so young, and the four men – Sir Geoffrey Miller had to be the one in the light jacket in the middle of the group, he was the oldest one there, and Morane was paying him special attention. A couple of red setters lay on the terrace steps.

Bennie sat there in his handy tree until the party showed signs of breaking up. The women went inside, and Morane and Sir Geoffrey walked up and down the terrace, talking and nodding at each other. Bennie hadn't brought his bag with him because this was meant to be a reconnaissance and it wasn't his custom to take a walk in the country with a gun in a bag unless he was sure he was going to use it.

In any case, there were snags – his view was too narrow, there were bits of masonry in the way, stone tubs with flowers. He needed another tree with a wider angle.

Now if they came down along one of the paths across the grass, maybe to stroll down to the river – that would be it. Tomorrow he could wait all day. All he wanted was a fair view of Aloysius Morane, just long enough to take proper care of him, and tuck him away.

He began to check the area for a better tree. Sir Geoffrey and Morane had gone into the house. But then the young girl came out and started chucking a ball about on the grass for the setters to chase after, and she was wandering across the grass too near where Bennie sat in his tree. He could hear her laughing and the panting of those dogs as they raced about. There wasn't all that much cover, and if she happened to glance up she had to see him. This was the kind of thing you couldn't allow for. Bennie didn't dare move on his perch.

She didn't notice him, she was having too much fun with her dogs, and as soon as she began to head down to the landing stage Bennie made a sharp descent from his tree because he reckoned he'd pushed his luck as far as it might go. Once he had waited two days and a night in a freezing old ruin to make a hit, living on cold coffee and fruit.

Squatting in a tree would be no punishment. If Morane stayed at *River Bank House* just for a couple of days, he had to come out and make a target of himself, sometime or other. He wouldn't spend all the time inside the house talking money with Sir Geoffrey Miller.

He followed the course of the wall down towards the river, looking for a nice easy tree with an open view of the house. And no obstructions like barbed wire in the way of a quick exit.

The wall ended short of the water; there was a tangle of bushes and reeds, and then the bank. He now had the house in full view, but he was far more interested in the sight he had of the girl. She must have changed in the boat-house. She stood balancing herself on the edge of the landing stage in a red bikini while the dogs sported about in the water. He guessed she was about seventeen or so, nicely put together. She did a neat dive and the dogs paddled around her and barked happily.

She swam upstream, not thirty yards from where he crouched in the bushes, and he was wishing it was Morane out there: he had the automatic under his arm and at that range he could sink Morane without any further sweat.

He let the girl get out of sight around the bend in the river, and started back.

He was not terribly happy when he reached the Cortina and saw another car parked there on the roadside, and he was distinctly peeved when he recognised the two men in the car.

'I don't need you here,' he said sharply. 'What's the idea?'

'Perhaps a progress report might be in order,' said Ambrose Halder.

'Checking up on me, is that it?' Bennie demanded. 'I'm busy.'

'I hope you are,' said Halder mildly. 'I am not interfering. You have seen Morane in there?'

'I have. I'm not here for the country air, or the scenery. I've seen him all right. And I don't need you pushing me.'

Having made his point, Bennie was about to get into his car when Halder called him back.

'You should know this, Mr Lucas – Morane will be at *River Bank House* three or four days. Mr Duchenne rang the Court Pavilion Hotel and that was what he was told. So that should give you time to plan your operation.'

'Good for Mr Duchenne,' said Bennie. 'He probably tipped them off that something was up, that wasn't a smart move.'

Tony smiled and shook his head. 'Give me credit for a little common sense, Bennie. I spoke to the reception girl, it was a routine business call, so stop agitating yourself, and the next time you have to leave your car while you go snooping I suggest you hide it in the bushes somewhere.'

'Are you telling me my business?' said Bennie.

'If you're any good and do your job,' said Tony, 'people might start remembering about cars that have been seen on the road-side around here. Where do you plan to spend the night? Sleeping rough? There's a room booked for you at the Datchford Arms in the name of Charlie Jones. But of course if you insist on being exclusive you won't hurt our feelings.'

'I just don't like working with a crowd at my elbow,' said Bennie. 'I don't need advice or supervision from anybody.'

'That is understood,' said Halder pleas-antly. 'You are the professional. Have you found a place that will suit your purpose?'

'The trees down there at the end of the wall,' said Bennie. 'Near the river, I can see over the wall. I'll get him.'

'You have three days,' said Halder. 'Then I

may hope for a result, Mr Lucas?'

'That's why I'm here,' said Bennie.

'I will be waiting for you in my room after dinner tonight,' said Halder, and now he was the boss giving orders. 'Room fourteen, at ten o'clock. There are matters to be settled between us.'

'Like money,' said Bennie.

'It is ready for collection,' said Halder. 'Make sure nobody sees you coming to my room.'

'I won't advertise it,' said Bennie.

'We have been here long enough,' said Halder.

Bennie watched them drive off towards the village. Then he began to look for a better spot to leave the Cortina, and it would not have to be too far away from where he planned to be working. He had a set of dummy number plates to use when it was done and he was on the way back, and he already knew the route he would take.

He checked on both sides of the road on foot. He found an untidy clump of trees with a rickety wooden field gate with rusty wire fastened to the top to keep it closed. Obviously the gate hadn't been opened for a long time, and the trees inside were straggly and overgrown.

There was plenty of room in there to park the Cortina, and it wouldn't be seen from the road.

When he drove into the village he took the fork that skirted the other side of the green opposite the pub; he wouldn't check in there until the last minute, and his luggage would be in the bag from the Cortina's boot. The three of them spending the night in the same pub was risky, but it seemed to be the only way he was going to latch on to that money.

Bennie never operated on credit. That was the surest way to find yourself running for cover with nothing in your pockets. Cash in advance. Always.

He drove across into Wallingford and had a good meal in a superior place right in the middle of the town where there was plenty of trade, and nobody would notice him, which was what he always wanted. He was happy to be the nondescript little man eating alone, the kind of customer busy waiters served last because they know he won't kick up a fuss.

14

Tony had waited all the evening to be invited to join the conference with Bennie Lucas in Halder's room. He and Halder had dined together, but it had been nothing like a social occasion. Just the minimum of talk. It was like eating with an elderly uncle who had a bad temper and very little regard for his younger companion. Before the meal was over Tony had concluded that his status had changed, now he was no more than an observer, an outsider and perhaps not to be trusted. There had been no sign of Bennie Lucas, and his name hadn't been mentioned.

When Halder finished his coffee he said a curt good-night and went upstairs, and there had been no invitation to come up and join him later. Tony thought about following him and in fact got as far as the foot of the stairs. Instead he went into the bar, which was being well patronised, largely by the cricketers from the Datchford club. Tony drank some slow whiskies and listened to the cheerful chat without really following much of it since cricket meant nothing to him. They were playing the Eton Ramblers the next week-end, apparently the big game of the season.

He missed seeing Bennie arrive at the hotel entrance, but when he checked the parking place at the rear the green Cortina was there. About half past ten he went upstairs and tapped at Halder's door. After a pause Halder opened the door slightly. He was still fully dressed, and there was no welcome on his face.

'May I come in?' said Tony softly.

'It would serve no purpose,' said Halder. 'You need concern yourself no longer. Thank you for your assistance. Good night, Mr Duchenne.' The door closed.

As a rejection that was definite enough. He was out. *'Thank you for your assistance'* – in other words, don't bother me any more.

He went back to his room along the corridor, and his immediate impulse was to pack his bag and leave then and there. He wasn't wanted, so to hell with them. He went downstairs and found the hotel office all locked up. Still simmering, he went for a walk around the green, his mind in a complete muddle.

He tramped and tramped, and when he was quieter and his leg had begun to complain, he went back and up to his bed. He would decide what he was going to do in the morning.

He was late down to breakfast, Halder wasn't there and neither was Bennie Lucas. He remembered Clara telling him that Halder didn't eat breakfast. That must have been a whole life-time away, at the *Villa Hermosa* stuck up there on the cliffs over the sea. He found that Bennie's car had gone. He waited until mid-morning and Halder hadn't come down.

Upstairs he found the maid doing Halder's room, and she told him she understood the room was vacant, the gentleman had left that morning. In the hotel office the manager informed him that his account had been settled. Halder had gone. Tony didn't ask about the room booked in the name of Charlie Jones – Halder would have paid for that as well. Very decent and gentlemanly of him.

Tony's car was still there, the car they had come down in. Halder couldn't drive with his arm in a sling still, so Bennie must have driven him, probably to a railway station to get him off the scene and back to London.

For a while Tony even played with the notion of ringing *River Bank House* and warning Morane to stay inside and keep out of the grounds for the next three days. Would it work? If Bennie couldn't do it here he would try again somewhere else. Halder had probably given him the money last night, and Bennie wasn't the type to give in easily.

Unable to make up his mind, Tony sat on a bench in the sunshine by the green. It was very peaceful and normal. A middle-aged lady was walking her poodle, a couple of young mothers with prams were taking their offspring for an airing, an elderly gentleman in a yellow straw hat was inspecting the cricket square.

Without quite knowing what he intended to do, Tony got into his car and drove along the road to where they had talked to Bennie the day before. Bennie had evidently taken his advice, he couldn't see the green Cortina anywhere. Perhaps Bennie was still driving Halder somewhere. Or he might be squatting up in a tree down there with his gun.

Tony began to follow the wall down in among the trees; there was no path and plenty of brambles and undergrowth, not easy walking, and in places the light was poor. He was watching the lower branches of the trees near the wall, not at all sure of the reception he might get if he found Bennie.

He wasn't being very cautious about his progress. He was in too much of a hurry, and his limp was no help. He guessed he couldn't be far from the river now. He halted for a moment and was about to light a cigarette.

A quiet voice over his head said, 'looking for somebody?'

Well hidden by the leafy branches, Bennie Lucas was peering down at him. Tony could have walked past without seeing him.

'You shouldn't be here,' said Bennie.

'Where's Halder?'

'He's not up here,' said Bennie. 'You don't catch on very fast, do you? He gave you the boot last night. You're out, so why don't you stay out? You're an embarrassment, Mr Duchenne, and that's the honest truth.'

Tony stared up at him. He could see Bennie's gun, a rifle with a slender barrel, wedged in a fork of the tree.

'Be a nice sensible man and push off,' said Bennie.

Tony began to climb the tree.

'Don't be daft,' said Bennie urgently. 'You'll mess it up–'

'I hope so,' said Tony. Bennie could easily have stopped him. He could have knocked him down with the butt of his rifle. He made hostile comments, he invited Tony to fall and break his goddam neck and stop interfering in what no longer concerned him, all in a fierce whisper. But he didn't actually do anything to dislodge him. In fact he retreated a little to make room.

'You're an obstinate bastard,' he said.

'I'll take that gun,' said Tony. 'The party is over.'

'Look,' said Bennie, parting the leaves, 'the party is just under way–'

There was an excellent view of the terrace. There were four people sitting around a table at lunch. It was no picnic. The sun glinted on silverware and glasses and there was a manservant in the background.

'That's Morane in the dark blazer with the shiny buttons,' said Bennie, 'and that's Sir Geoffrey Miller sitting opposite–'

'There's going to be no shooting while I'm around here,' said Tony, and reached for Bennie's rifle.

Bennie held him off. 'You're too late … now don't you go spoiling things – I'm only up here in case he misses … take a look down there by the river.'

Ambrose Halder had emerged from the shelter of the wall where it ended by the water. He was walking briskly up the grassy slope towards the terrace, dignified and erect, his right arm still in a sling.

'Good God!' said Tony.

'You open your mouth now and I'll let you have it.' Bennie had swung the barrel of his rifle round so that it all but scraped Tony's face. He closed his eyes and swallowed and he could feel the nausea beginning to surge inside him.

'I'll be quiet.'

'Good,' said Bennie. 'Watch this.'

The intruder had been noticed. Morane and his host had got to their feet and the servant was moving across the terrace. Morane evidently said something to Sir Geoffrey Miller and touched him on the shoulder, as though indicating that he would deal with the matter.

He went down the terrace steps on his own, and he was too far away for any expression on his face to be noticed, but he wasn't acting like a man with anything to fear.

He halted on the grass below the steps, his hands on his hips in a masterful and challenging posture.

Now Bennie had shifted his rifle so that he

had Morane covered. 'You have one hell of a surprise coming to you,' he murmured.

The two men met. Awkwardly Halder put his left hand in his pocket, and only then did Morane lunge forward. The automatic made little noise. Morane sagged to his knees, and then fell slowly on his face. One of the two women on the terrace screamed, but for a moment nobody up there moved.

Ambrose Halder took three sharp paces away, lowered his head and put the muzzle of the gun into his mouth. And this time the explosion was even more muted.

'That was the way he wanted it,' said Bennie. 'So I gave him the gun ... now we'd better get to hell out of here.'

'You arranged all this,' said Tony, scrambling down out of the tree. 'You knew he was going to kill himself–'

'Can you think of a smarter solution?' Bennie came rapidly down after him, darted into the bushes and brought out his bag; he took the rifle to pieces and packed it away. 'I made the occasion for him and he took it, he took it very nicely – like you, I was only a spectator ... didn't have to do a thing once I had set it up. And I got paid, last night.'

'So that makes it all right,' said Tony.

'You look kind of sick to me,' said Bennie.

'You shouldn't hang around here, you were seen at the pub with Halder, I wasn't, and you stayed at the same hotel in London. They'll be around asking some questions pretty soon. You should take a nice long trip out of the country.'

'But I had nothing to do with it at the end,' said Tony. 'I only came here to stop it.'

'Who's going to believe you?'

Bennie was moving with speed now, carrying his bag. Tony had to hurry to keep up with him.

'You can't involve me, chum,' said Bennie. 'I set it up but I didn't pull the trigger.'

'There are two dead men over that wall,' said Tony, 'and you can't pretend you're not morally responsible, and so am I–'

'Okay,' said Bennie. 'So go and give yourself up if it'll make you feel better, but don't come looking for me because I don't expect I'll be available. And you couldn't prove a thing on your own. I'd call it a nice tidy ending, Mr Duchenne.'

'Is there anything you wouldn't do for money?' said Tony.

'This is a funny time to start giving me a sermon,' said Bennie. 'Halder got what he wanted and he took the only way out. No fuss for you or me – he shoots Morane and then commits suicide – it's perfect.'

'It's perfect all right,' said Tony, 'from your point of view.'

'Now don't you go awkward on me,' said Bennie. 'It's too late, the job's over. So you can stick that so-called conscience of yours in cold storage, and we'll both get to hell out of here while there's time.'

They were coming to the end of the wood. Through the trees they saw a police car flash past in the direction of *River Bank House*.

Bennie gave Tony a very sharp look. 'You were never right for this business,' he said. 'The old man was serious, but you just messed about on the outside. So what's it going to be now? Are you going to run along there like a good little boy with clean hands and say your piece?'

Tony was leaning against a tree trunk. He wiped his face.

'You look lousy,' said Bennie. 'Are you going to stir up trouble?'

'There wouldn't be any point now, would there?' Tony straightened up.

'Good,' said Bennie. 'Nice and tidy.'

And that was the way it was.

The publishers hope that this book has given you enjoyable reading. Large Print Books are especially designed to be as easy to see and hold as possible. If you wish a complete list of our books please ask at your local library or write directly to:

Dales Large Print Books
Magna House, Long Preston,
Skipton, North Yorkshire.
BD23 4ND